HOCKEYBAT HARRIS

Geoffrey Bilson

with the assistance of the

**Saskatchewan
Arts Board**

Hockeybat Harris

by Geoffrey Bilson

Kids Can Press

Cover photography from the Toronto Telegram Photographic Collection, York University Archives. Every reasonable effort has been made to trace ownership of and give accurate credit to copyrighted material. Information that would enable the publisher to correct any discrepancies in future editions would be appreciated.

Kids Can Press acknowledges with appreciation the special assistance and support of the Saskatchewan Arts Board in the production of this book and the financial support of the Ontario Arts Council, the Canada Council for the Arts and the Government of Canada, through the BPIDP, for our publishing activity.

Published in Canada by
Kids Can Press Ltd.
29 Birch Avenue
Toronto, ON M4V 1E2

Published in the U.S. by
Kids Can Press Ltd.
2250 Military Road
Tonawanda, NY 14150

www.kidscanpress.com

Cover design by Franklin Hammond
Printed and bound in Canada

CM PA 84 0 9 8 7 6

Canadian Cataloguing in Publication Data

Bilson, Geoffrey, 1938–1987
  Hockeybat Harris

ISBN 0-919964-57-5

I. Title.

PS8553.I47H62 1984   jC813'.54   C84-09872-3
PZ7.BhhHO 1984

Kids Can Press is a ʟ◯ʀ∪S™ Entertainment company

For David, Elizabeth and Jonathan

CHAPTER 1

THE whole house smelled of polish when Bob Williams came home for lunch one hot day in August. Mrs. Williams was sitting at the kitchen table looking flushed and tired, but she jumped up when Bob came in.

"Come on, Bob. Give me a hand with the piano."

Bob followed his mother into the front room. Everything was spotless. It was like spring cleaning time.

"What's going on, mum?" Bob asked as they tugged the piano away from the wall.

"...mmh...tidying...." Mrs. Williams had disappeared behind the piano with the vacuum cleaner. Bob had to wait until she surfaced before he could understand what she was saying.

"Just tidying up a bit. The evacuee committee is meeting here this afternoon. We have to discuss some of the arrangements. The children are arriving about three o'clock from Regina."

"You mean we'll get one today? Right here?"

"Well not today." Mrs. Williams motioned to him to help her push the piano back in place. She coiled up the vacuum cleaner cord, while looking around the room one last time.

"But you said we would get one as soon as they came. How long do we have to wait?"

"We'll see. They've decided to put the children in the Deaf School for a couple of days. The doctors will check them and they'll have a chance to rest from the trip. They've been travelling for weeks, you know."

"Ah, mum, why don't they just send us a kid? I'm fed up waiting."

Weeks ago, Mrs. Williams had received a letter from the evacuee committee to say that they had been approved as a home for a guest child. Ever since then, Bob had been waiting anxiously for someone to arrive. The *Star-Phoenix* was full of news about the war, the Battle of Britain, and the plans that the Germans had to invade Britain, but weeks passed and no children arrived in Saskatoon. Now they were here.

Mrs. Williams smiled at Bob as she wheeled the vacuum cleaner back to the kitchen.

"Well, we've been waiting months already," she said, "so I expect we can wait a day or two more. At least they're safely here now."

"Do you think he'll come here next week?" Bob asked as they ate their lunch.

"Now don't get your hopes up, dear. There are only thirty children coming today and we may not be chosen to take one this time. We might have to wait for some of the later arrivals."

"Aw, mum, you're on the committee. Why shouldn't one of them come here?"

"Oh, it all depends," Mrs. Williams sounded vague. "We'll just have to see."

After lunch Bob cycled up Clarence Avenue to the schoolyard, glad to get out of the house before his mother could think of more work for him to do. The schoolyard looked the same as it had for as long as Bob could remember. The grass was burned brown and there were big dirt patches around the baseball diamond that sent dust flying into the air with every puff of wind. Behind the plate, the wire netting hung loosely from a rickety wooden frame. A few trees on Eleventh Street threw some shade over one side of the field but most of it lay open to the hot sun. Now that the summer was coming to an end, there were more boys playing here, and the lucky ones who had been away to camp or the lake had begun to come home.

This was the first summer of the war, but to Bob, it was the same as every other summer. Sometimes it was hard to remember that a war was on. The stories in the newspaper were about places so far away that Bob had trouble believing they were real. But everyone he knew had an uncle or a brother or a father in the forces. His own Uncle Arthur was in the RCN. Bob and his friend Danny Miller often cycled to the airport on the edge of town to watch the men there building a huge base where pilots from all over the world would train.

"And now I'm going to get a brother who's been right in the war," Bob thought. "I bet he'll have some swell stories."

Danny Miller was sitting in the shade when Bob flopped down beside him.

"Hi, Danny. Today's the day. Mum says the Brits are coming this afternoon."

"So you'll get your brother?" Danny smiled. "Do you think he'll know how to play ball?"

"It's all cricket over there, isn't it? We'll have to teach him."

"If he wants. Maybe he'll be one of those fat guys with glasses." Danny blew out his cheeks and crossed his eyes.

"Oh swell. You mean the war could go on for years and he'd be lying around the house like a blob."

"Yeah, could be. Drinking tea."

"And eating brussels sprouts. Everyone says Brits always eat brussels sprouts."

"A fat guy with glasses, drinking tea and eating brussels sprouts. Wish I had a brother like that," Danny grinned.

"Gee, do you think he could be like that, really?" Bob asked, suddenly serious. "I mean, what'd I do with someone like that?"

"Sure, they might send you some little kid, or even a nice little girl — a sister."

"They wouldn't!"

Danny grinned at Bob, then jumped up to take his turn at bat. Bob joined in the game, but it was hard to keep his mind on it. Danny had made jokes at other times about the kind of brother Bob might get. Now that the children had arrived, Bob felt worried for the first time. "What if the committee does send us a little kid, or a girl. Nah — they wouldn't." Bob told himself again, "Mum told them what she wanted. And she's on the committee."

Just before three, Bob drifted over to where Danny was playing in the outfield.

"I want to see those kids. You want to come down to the station?"

"Well, I don't know," Danny hesitated, staring into the centre of the field watching the play.

"Ah, come on, this is getting boring. And we could have a soda on the way back."

"Okay." Danny sounded reluctant, but he followed Bob off the field.

The boys cycled over University Bridge and headed toward the railway tracks. Neither of them said anything and Bob was aware of the tension between them that he had felt recently. He could not explain it to himself, but lately Danny seemed angry about things he never explained. Bob looked at his friend, cycling along beside him staring straight ahead,

11

wrapped up in his own thoughts. Something was on Danny's mind right now, but Bob could not guess what it was.

As the boys turned onto First Avenue, they could see a big crowd outside the station. It spread out along the sidewalk from the entrance. People crowded around the door and a couple of policemen were making sure that the road in front of the station was not blocked. Cars were parked in a line, their drivers leaning on the hoods, smoking and chatting to each other.

"What's going on?" Bob asked.

"Looks like someone big's coming to town."

The boys propped their bikes against the wall and began to wriggle and push their way through the crowd. It was hard work as the crowd was packed together. Even when Bob said, "Excuse me — I've got a train to catch," not many people moved. Danny gave up and went back to sit by the bikes and wait for Bob.

When Bob did get into the station hall, it was jammed with people and stiflingly hot. It took him a few minutes to squeeze through to the platform. He was glad to be outside in the breeze. There was a space by the wall at the top of the stairs which led to the passageway under the tracks, and Bob settled into it. He looked around for Danny, but the crowd was so thick that Bob could not see very far. Everyone was in good spirits; a hum of voices and the sound of laughter surrounded him.

"What's everyone waiting for, ma'am?" Bob asked a tall woman who was fanning herself with a magazine.

"Why, for the guest children. They're coming today. Up from Regina."

"All these people?"

"The biggest crowd since the King and Queen came through last year," the woman said proudly, as if she had organized the reception herself.

"And the Mayor's here," a woman next to her said. "I saw him when I got here. Those kiddies will really have a warm Saskatoon welcome."

"And they deserve it after everything they've been through."

Bob was amazed that so many people had turned out just to see some kids from Britain arrive in Saskatoon. It was a long time before the train arrived. Finally, after covering the crowd with a cloud of smoke and steam, it squealed to a halt. There was a long pause while everyone craned to look over the tracks. Bob could only see the top of the cars, so he turned around and looked down the stairs into the tunnel.

"There they are!" someone shouted, and the crowd began to cheer.

A minute or so later a couple of men came up the stairs from the tunnel, leading two small boys by the hand. The boys wore grey flannel shorts, black blazers, shirts and ties and they had raincoats over their arms. More children followed. All of them were pale and most of them looked very tired. The crowd began to clap and cheer as the children appeared. The noise startled some of the smaller children who hesitated, looking confused.

"Stand back please — let the little ones through," a policeman ordered, pushing his way through the crowd.

A girl about Bob's age paused on the stairs waiting for room. She wore a faded, print dress and a cardboard box was slung over one shoulder. The girl turned to one of the adults leading the children and said, "Is that a bomb shelter?"

"What, dear?"

"That tunnel we just came through — do you use it as a bomb shelter?"

"Why no, dear. We don't need bomb shelters here."

"Ooh, aren't you lucky. We slept in one every night when we were at home."

"Well, that's one thing you won't have to worry about here, dear," the woman said with a smile. "That's why you're here."

The policeman and the escorts opened up a path through the crowd and the party began to move. Lots of women wanted to kiss the smaller children and people patted the children as they went past. When the reporter from the *Star-Phoenix* tried to take a small girl by the hand, she screamed and began to cry. The reporter looked embarrassed and shouted, "Now then, who would like their picture taken? See yourself in the paper, send it home to mum and dad."

A little blonde girl was persuaded to go to the Mayor. He lifted her up and the crowd cheered again. The girl did not smile, but looked down at the crowd solemnly and put her thumb in her mouth.

"Well, isn't she sweet. Just like Shirley Temple," the reporter said as his flash went off.

After a short speech by the Mayor, the children were led through the noisy crowd to First Avenue. There they were divided into groups and put into the cars which were waiting for them. By the time Bob reached the street, the last child was getting into a car. The crowd gave one last cheer and the cars drove off. People stood around talking and looking pleased, as if they had been to a ball game and seen their team win.

Bob found Danny sitting by the bikes, his arms wrapped around his knees and staring at the ground. Bob was surprised that Danny looked so glum when everyone else seemed so happy.

"Hey, Danny, what happened to you?"

"Nothing. Just too many people."

"That was some crowd. Did you see the Brits?"

"Yeah, I saw them."

"I got real close — one of them said she slept in a bomb shelter every night. I bet she's glad to be over here."

"Oh, sure they're lucky. Thirty of them — real lucky." Danny's voice was thick and he sounded as if

15

he were trying not to cry. Bob knelt down by his friend.

"What's wrong, Danny? What happened?"

"Look, I didn't want to come here, you know. I should have played ball instead."

"But that was some crowd. You don't see one like that in Saskatoon everyday. Aren't you glad you saw it?"

"Yeah, they'll turn out for some nice British kids," Danny snarled.

"Come on, Danny. What's bugging you?"

"I'll bet you something."

"What?"

"I'll bet you not one of them's Jewish."

Danny stared straight at Bob, and his eyes were hard and angry.

"What do you mean?" Bob asked uneasily.

"None of those kids is Jewish. My uncle and some of the profs at the varsity have been trying for years and years to get refugees over here. The government won't let them in because they're Jewish."

"Ah, come on. What difference does that make?"

"Are you calling me a liar?" Danny shouted. "It's true, ask Mr. King. He doesn't care what they're doing to people over there. And where were all these people when my uncle started his committee?" Danny waved at the groups standing on the sidewalk. "But they'll all come and cheer nice British Christians." Danny was sobbing and the tears began to run down his face. He wiped his face with his arm, then jumped up and grabbed his bike.

Bob watched Danny ride away. He was stunned by his friend's anger. It took Bob a moment to recover and begin to chase Danny. He caught up to him after a few blocks, but as Bob drew alongside, Danny tried to ride faster.

"Just go away, Bob. Leave me alone."

There seemed to be nothing else to do, so Bob left his friend and rode on up the bridge. He stopped at the top of Broadway Bridge to let a streetcar rumble by. When he turned and looked back, Danny was leaning against the parapet of the bridge, his head resting on the concrete as he stared out along the river. He looked very lonely.

It was some time before Mrs. Williams came home, and Bob met her at the door.

"Mum, do you know what Danny said?"

"Give me a moment to get into the house, Bob. What's so important?"

"We were at the station, watching the Brits. And Danny said none of them were Jewish."

"Why did he say that?" Mrs. Williams asked as she pulled the hatpin from her hat and shook out her hair.

"He says his uncle's been on a committee trying to get refugees into the country, but the government won't let them come because they're Jewish."

"Hitler's doing such terrible things. I'm sure Danny can't be right."

"But Danny was really mad. He was crying and

everything. He said no one helped his uncle but they all came to meet British kids."

"I do know there was a committee before the war," Mrs. Williams said, "and some of them are working with us now. We have people on our lists who will take in Jewish children. We have to put children in homes that are the same religion as their own, you see."

"But Danny says the government won't let them in. His uncle wouldn't lie, would he?"

"Of course not. I don't know what to think, Bob."

"Suppose we wrote and asked Mr. King. Would he tell us?"

Mrs. Williams looked surprised at the idea of writing to the Prime Minister, but she was soon convinced that it was worth trying and Bob sat down to write the letter.

> Dear Mr. King,
> My friend Danny says Jewish children can't come to Canada. Is this true? I think it is unfair, they are being bombed and put in concentration camps. We should let all kinds of children come to Canada. Please let them in.
>
> > Yours sincerely,
> > Robert Williams

"That's good and clear," Mrs. Williams said. "Address it to the Right Honourable William Lyon

Mackenzie King, House of Commons, Ottawa and drop it in the mail. And let's hope he has the right answer."

Bob walked back from the mail box, kicking a stone along the street. It had been a strange day. Only once before had he seen a crowd like the one at the station. Then Danny was so mad and unhappy. Maybe he wouldn't want to talk to Bob again. Tomorrow was Sunday and Bob would have to wait until after church before he could go and see Danny. Maybe he should even wait a day or two.

"No, I'll go and see him tomorrow. I'll tell him I've written to the Prime Minister. Maybe that'll help."

CHAPTER 2

SUNDAY was hot and sunny, the sort of day on which Bob hated to go to church. Today, especially, he wanted to go to see Danny, but there was no escape and Bob had to go with his parents. He was all dressed up in his best pants, with his hair carefully combed. Next week, choir would start meeting again. It was one more sign that the summer was nearly over.

The bell was ringing as they reached St. James and they hurried up the steps and into the church.

"Good morning, Bob," Mrs. McIntosh, the choir mistress said. "We'll see you at Thursday practice, I hope?"

"Yes, Mrs. McIntosh."

"That's good. We may have some new members. I think some of the British children will be joining. They're all here today, you know."

As he settled into his seat in the church, Bob could see the British children sitting in the first two pews.

There were about thirty of them. The boys' hair was as carefully combed as Bob's and many of them wore black blazers. The girls were all wearing freshly ironed dresses. Some of the younger children were twisting around to look at the congregation. There was a low murmur of conversation in the church and it was obvious that people were talking about the guest children. The older children knew it too, as they sat stiffly in their places. As soon as the first hymn was announced, they jumped to their feet, glad to have something to do.

After the service, the congregation went to the church hall to meet the children and their escorts. Bob went with his parents. The churchwomen had made cakes and cookies and big jugs of lemonade. The guest children stood in small groups near the tables, eating quickly, as if they had not had the chance to eat so many cookies in a long time.

"That's right, dears, eat up," Mrs. McIntosh said as she came from the kitchen with a large teapot in her hands. "There's plenty for everyone."

"I guess that includes me?" Bob said.

"Don't spoil your lunch," Mrs. McIntosh replied sharply.

Greg Rogers was chatting to one of the English girls as they stood by the table. Greg was in grade seven but he had been held back a couple of years. At school, Greg was dangerous to cross, quick with his fists and ready to take advantage of his size. Bob always felt nervous around Greg and he had been very relieved when Greg had dropped out of the choir a year ago. It had been no fun having Greg around after choir practice. Bob supposed that Mrs. Rogers kept bringing Greg to church in the hope that he would change. It had not worked yet. Bob turned away, but Greg noticed him and called, "Hey, Bob, get on over here and meet Doris."

"Hi, Greg."

"Tell Bob how you like Canada, Doris."

"Ooh, it's lovely," the girl said in a funny accent. Then she giggled in embarrassment.

"Bob, can you guess where she's from?"

"No, Greg," Bob said, hoping he could get away soon. He felt like a fool standing there so Greg could show off to him.

"I can't say it, can I, Doris? You tell him."

"Middlesborough."

"Yeah, that's it. Crazy name, eh, Bob?"

The girl giggled again nervously. Bob felt awkward. He could never talk to girls — not that he particularly wanted to — but he always blushed when he tried. He blushed now, and Greg laughed. He seemed to enjoy making Bob uncomfortable, but luckily, he seemed more interested in Doris. He gave Bob a gentle push. "See you around, Bob. Me and Doris have some things to talk about."

Bob walked off quickly. Most of the guest children were lost in crowds of adults and the roar of conversation filled the hall and echoed off the high wooden walls and ceiling. Even though the windows and doors were open, it was very hot inside. Bob looked for his parents, hoping they were ready to go home for lunch. Mrs. Williams was busy talking to some children and Bob could not see his father in the crowd. He headed for the door to wait for them outside. As he squeezed between a group of adults and the table, which was now almost bare of food and littered with empty cups and glasses, Bob stumbled and bumped into a boy.

"Watch what you're doing," the boy said angrily.

"Sorry, I tripped."

"Not enough just to look, is it? You have to poke the animals, do you? Feeding time at the zoo?"

The boy was about Bob's age, but shorter and slighter. His dark hair showed no sign of the combing it had been given before church, but flew in all directions. His two front teeth looked too big for his face. He had high cheekbones and large ears that jutted out from his head. His dark brown eyes were angry and his face bright red from the heat. Bob almost expected him to start pawing the ground like an angry elephant getting ready to charge.

"Zoo? Who are you? Dumbo the elephant?"

"Oh I say, how comic. You should work for Arthur Askey."

"Who's he? What's got you so mad anyway? I said I was sorry."

"Quiet, boys," one of the church ladies said. "The rector's going to say a few words. You can have a nice chat afterwards."

The rector stood on the stage holding up his hands for silence. Out of the corner of his eye, Bob watched the English boy while the rector spoke about the generous offer thousands of Canadians had made to open their homes to evacuees from Britain.

"Those few we have amongst us today are, we trust, just the first of many hundreds yet to come to safety. I know you have all done your best to make them feel welcome this morning. I am glad to tell you that the children will now be going to the Gem Cafe where Mr. Chronos will give them a real Canadian lunch. Afterwards, they will tour the town and visit the forestry farm. I'm sure we'll see a number of them at St. James in the near future. And now, let us pray."

The English boy had been scowling while the rector spoke. When people began to talk again, he spun around and caught hold of Bob's arm.

"Do you think I didn't see you staring at me? What d'you expect — tricks?"

"Sure," Bob snapped. "Do you do them here?"

"Why don't you come outside and see?" The boy clenched his fists. He looked ridiculous glaring up at Bob. Bob looked down at him and grinned. At that moment, one of the matrons in charge of the children came by and said, "Come along, David. You'll have to say goodbye to your Canadian friend for now. The cars are waiting for us."

"I'll show you my tricks some other time."

"Sure, David."

"Well, isn't that nice," the woman said as she led David away. "Children make friends so quickly."

Bob grinned as he watched David being led from the hall. "I wonder if they're all like him," he thought. Bob followed the crowd to the line of cars that were waiting at the curb. As the British children were being organized into groups, Bob saw David shove one of the boys in his group.

"Watch out, Harris," the boy said.

David Harris pushed him again and they began scuffling. One of the men from the church stopped them and sent David off to join another group. Some of the children waved as the cars pulled away and one or two people on the curb clapped.

"I saw you talking to a couple of the children, dear. How did you like them?" Mrs. Williams asked as they walked home.

"I suppose they're okay, mum. I didn't really talk to any of them much. One guy was a bit of a jerk."

"I spoke to a couple of very nice girls — and a boy about your age. He seemed very polite. In fact, they all seem very well behaved."

"You know what I noticed, Mary?" Mr. Williams said. "I was amazed at the number of children Bob's age who had teeth missing."

"Do they play hockey, dad?"

"No, Bob. These were girls as well as boys."

"A lot of people noticed," Mrs. Williams said. "I asked one of the matrons about it."

"Is it something to do with the war, mum?"

"She said that some of the parents were so worried that their children wouldn't be let into Canada with bad teeth that they took them to the dentist to have them out before the doctor examined them. Can you imagine?"

"Why didn't they fill them?" Mr. Williams asked.

"Because it was cheaper to pull them, and quicker. They were afraid they'd miss their turn to come if they failed the medical. What is the world coming to, Ted?"

"Mum, if people want to get away from Britain that much, what's it like in places like France, now that the Germans are there?"

"It's hard to imagine, Bob, but people must be really desperate. I'm afraid there's not much hope of them getting out now."

"You mean they should have left before Hitler invaded?"

"That's how it looks, doesn't it, son?" Mr. Williams said as they walked toward their house.

"What if there's nowhere to go, dad?"

"There's always somewhere."

After lunch, Bob changed and got his bike. He rode slowly toward the river. He was thinking about all the people at church that morning. They had all been so glad to see the British kids. The ladies had baked the cakes and cookies. Right now, the kids would be finishing one of Mr. Chronos's great meals. Bob had been to the Gem Cafe once and he remembered the chocolate pie. Everyone was being so generous and helpful. The childrens' parents had sent them away, sure that someone would take care of them until the war was over. And they were right; people would take care of the children.

"But if Danny's right, there isn't always somewhere to go if you're in trouble," Bob thought. "Not when everyone you ask says no."

Bob stopped and looked down over the river from the corner of Saskatchewan Crescent. He suddenly felt nervous about going to Danny's. Maybe it would be better to wait a couple of days, just in case Danny was still mad or embarrassed by yesterday's scene. "That's stupid," Bob thought, beginning to cycle again. "Why waste an afternoon alone, especially with school starting soon."

CHAPTER 3

BOB stood on the pedals and pumped his way up the hill on Avenue A. At the top, he relaxed and rode easily over the crest. Soon he was on the highway and he could see the airport straight ahead. Even though it was Sunday, men and machines were at work, racing to lengthen the runways and build huts and hangars. In a month, the airport would be a training school for pilots, like the one in Prince Albert where Fred Miller was an instructor. The airport was one of Danny's favourite spots and Bob had not been surprised when Mrs. Miller told him that Danny had gone there.

Bob found Danny's bike propped up against the wire fence where the boys usually left them. Bob scrambled up a rise and saw Danny sitting on a large rock staring at the clouds of dust thrown up by the graders. Bob did not say anything, but he sat down on the ground, resting against the rock. He felt nervous. His stomach was tense and his mouth was dry. Danny glanced down at Bob, then looked away over the fence. For a long time the boys sat in silence.

At last Bob broke the silence, trying to sound casual. "They're really getting that hangar up. They'd only poured the foundation last time we were here." When Danny did not reply, Bob asked, "What'll they put in there?"

"Fred says they'll have Harvards and some twin engined planes — Ansons, he says," Danny said slowly. Planes always got him talking and Bob found himself grinning nervously with relief.

"I bet that'll be swell. Do you think they'll let us come and watch when they start training? I'd really like to watch them train, wouldn't you?"

"Yeah, they do formation flying and stuff. But they might be worried about spies, you know."

"We don't look like spies," Bob laughed.

"What do spies look like?"

It was a good question. People had been talking about spies and fifth columnists ever since the war began. Some men had been arrested on suspicion of spying in towns near Saskatoon. But Bob had never seen a picture of a real spy. In comics they usually had cloaks and big hats. Bob tried to imagine someone walking around Saskatoon dressed like that and he laughed.

"I guess they look foreign — you know — different."

Danny did not reply. Suddenly the tension between them heightened and Bob realized that he had said something wrong. Bob could hear Danny's shoes scrape on the rock just above his head and a small shower of dust rolled down by Bob's shoulder. Bob half turned to see if Danny was leaving, but Danny was sitting as he had at the station, with his knees drawn up and his arms around them. When Danny spoke, his voice was tight and thin.

"Yeah, some people do look foreign. Just one look at them and you know they're different."

Bob scrambled to his feet and turned to face Danny. Standing like this, Bob was eye to eye with his friend. Danny did not look at him but stared past Bob's head toward the airport. Suddenly Bob felt angry. He had come here hoping Danny would be back to normal but Danny was in one of his moods again. It made Bob feel that he was being blamed for something he had not done and he burst out, "What are you mad about now? What have I done?"

"Nothing," Danny said, not looking at him.

"What are you so moody about all the time? You act like a jerk sometimes, Danny."

"So get lost. No one asked you to come here."

The two boys stared at each other, then Danny looked away. Bob's face felt stiff and he was mad and miserable at the same time. He did not want to go.

"Danny..."

Danny turned his head away, resting his cheek on his knees. Bob stood with his fists clenched, then he let his hands relax.

"Come on, Danny. Why're you so mad? I didn't mean anything about you."

Danny still said nothing, but sat motionless, his face hidden. Bob shifted awkwardly from foot to foot. Then he shrugged his shoulders.

"Okay, Danny. I'll see you around." Bob took a step back, turning to go, but his heel caught in a tangle of dry grass and he tumbled over. His head hit the ground with a thump, his left elbow banged down on a rock, and Bob yelled with pain. Blood began to pour from the cut on his arm as Bob lay half stunned on the ground. Danny looked down from his rock, shocked, and then scrambled down to Bob's side.

"Bob, Bob, are you okay? Can you sit up?"

"Jeez, that hurts. I think I busted my arm."

"Let's have a look. Have you got a handkerchief?"

Danny made a bandage out of their handkerchiefs and managed to stop the bleeding. It hurt while he tied the bandage on, but since Bob could move his arm, they decided it was not broken. Danny helped Bob sit and propped him up against the rock.

"Thanks, Danny."

"You're welcome."

The polite reply sounded funny to both of them and they began to giggle.

"Anytime you fall on your head," Danny spluttered.

"Ouch," Bob winced, "it really hurts."

It took them a while to stop their nervous giggling.

They finally calmed down and sat side by side against the rock. Bob was content to sit there with his eyes closed while his head cleared. When he opened his eyes, he turned to Danny and said, "I didn't mean you, you know. Not when I said that stuff about people being different."

"Yeah I know, it's just..."

"You were really mad yesterday. I was worried."

"It just got to me. That big crowd for those kids. And no one bothered about my cousins."

"I was thinking about that at church. The Brits were there and all the ladies were there with cakes and stuff. Everyone was really nice. I mean no one that we know would tell a kid to get lost."

"Other people do, though. There are people who don't like us, like Greg Rogers."

"He's just dumb. Danny, I wrote to the Prime Minister, you know."

"What about?"

"About what you said — the committee and not letting your cousins come and all that."

"Do you think he'll answer you?" Danny laughed. "He never writes to my uncle."

"Yeah, well..." Bob shrugged and the two boys sat silently and stared across the airfield.

The noise of the machines stopped. It was late afternoon and the men were quitting for the day. The dust blew across the airport and it was suddenly very quiet. Danny pulled up a dry stalk of grass and began to shred it.

"You know, our family's been in Canada longer than lots of people around here."

"So?"

"My brother's in the air force. I've got cousins in the forces."

"My uncle's in the navy, Danny. Everyone's got someone in the forces."

"So then something like this refugee stuff comes along. It makes you think people don't really think you're Canadian at all."

"I do," Bob protested, puzzled by what Danny was saying.

"One of my cousins tried to go to Palestine."

"What for?"

"He says it's the only place a Jew can call his home."

"Do you want to go?"

"No. I like it here. I just get so mad sometimes."

"Yeah..."

"You know what one of my uncles says? He says it's like being a stranger in your own land. He says things are okay for a long time, then something happens. He says you realize you're an outsider."

"Do you feel that way, Danny?"

"Sometimes, Bob."

"That must be awful," Bob said slowly, turning to look at Danny. "How come you never talked about it before?"

"You can't talk about it to everyone. Look, we'd better go or my mum will get real mad. Can you ride home?"

"Sure."

The boys rode home together, coasting down the long hill past the Normal School. "What's normal about wanting to be a teacher?" they joked as they often did when they passed the school. Now the student teachers were sharing the space with air force trainees.

"If the war's still on when I'm old enough, I'm going to join the navy," Bob said.

"Why? Why not learn to fly. That's the best thing..."

"...Fred says." Bob laughed and Danny laughed with him.

As the boys cycled slowly up Broadway Bridge, a line of cars passed them. The British children were returning from their day out. They looked excited and happy, many of them pointing and waving at the people walking on the bridge. The pedestrians smiled and waved back at the children. Bob and Danny watched as the cars turned and headed toward the Deaf School.

"Looks like you could have your English brother tomorrow," Danny said.

"Yeah, I met a couple of them this morning. Greg Rogers was showing off to some girl, and I nearly had a fight with one of the guys."

"What'd you do?"

"I don't know. He just wanted to start something."

"You're not having much luck today, are you?" Danny laughed. "Everyone's getting angry at you these days."

"Just so you don't stay mad."

Bob felt much happier as he cycled home from Danny's. Even though his arm hurt and he had a headache, Bob was glad he had fallen over. Now he and Danny were talking again and Bob could understand a bit about how his friend felt. He ran up the steps and pushed the door open. The door was never locked.

CHAPTER 4

"WHATEVER have you been doing?" Mrs. Williams asked.

"Nothing, mum. I fell, that's all. It's just a cut."

"Let me look."

Mrs. Williams removed the bandages, then brought a bowl of water to the table. Bob winced as she washed the cut.

"Ah, mum, it's nothing really. Don't make a fuss about it."

"I'll be the judge of that," Mrs. Williams said firmly. Secretly, Bob felt glad to be fussed over.

"Whatever will you do when you've two to look after, Mary? You'll be worn out in a week," Mr. Williams said.

"I can look after two as well as I do one — you can be sure of that."

"I am sure, love," Mr. Williams smiled.

After supper they all went into the yard. The evenings were getting shorter now, but it was still light enough for Bob and his father to throw a baseball. After asking Bob how he felt, Mrs. Williams settled down to watch them play. She reached into her bag and pulled out some knitting. She spent a lot of her free time knitting for the men in the forces and Bob was now used to seeing khaki and blue wool instead of the bright colours she had knitted with before the war.

"Series will start soon," Mr. Williams said. He had pitched for his home town years ago and baseball was still his favourite sport.

"It would be swell to see a game, eh, dad?"

"Well, at least it's on the radio. We didn't have that when I was a boy."

"I wish the radio had pictures, like the newsreels, so you didn't have to wait to see it in the theatre."

"I'm sure they will one day," Mrs. Williams said. "I was reading about it in the paper — a piece about the world's fair in New York. What do they call it? Television, that's it."

"Science fiction, Mary," Mr. Williams laughed.

"That's what your mother said about the radio, Ted," Mrs. Williams said, "and now you can't get her away from the soap operas."

Bob laughed. His grandmother's passion for the soaps on the American radio was a family joke. Gran even wrote letters to the shows giving the characters advice. She would not believe that they were just actors. His parents laughed too, and the happy sound filled the small yard. Bob liked these summer evenings at home. Some of his earliest memories were of playing ball with his father who had hoped, from the day Bob could stand up, to make him into a pitcher. Mr. Williams had not given up hope completely, but it was fading.

"Maybe my brother will make a better pitcher for you."

"Wouldn't be hard, eh, Bob?"

"Don't be cruel to the boy, Ted."

Later in the evening as they were sitting in the house, the telephone rang. Mr. Williams turned down the radio while Mrs. Williams went to answer the phone. She came back, looking upset.

"Mary, what's the matter?" Mr. Williams asked.

"That was Mrs. Smith, from the committee. She says all the children have been quarantined. One of them has scarlet fever. He's in City Hospital."

"That's nasty, Mary. How long will they be in quarantine?"

"About ten days."

"Ten days!" Bob exclaimed. "I can't wait that long, mum. I thought we'd have him here tomorrow."

"It'll be longer than ten days I'm afraid, Bob."

"What d'you mean, Mary?" Mr. Williams sounded concerned.

"We aren't getting anyone from this group."

The room was quiet as Bob and his father looked blankly at Mrs. Williams.

"Why not, mum? Why aren't we going to get one? I mean, you're on the committee and everything. Don't you get first choice or something?"

"It doesn't work like that, Bob. They try to match the children to the homes. I suppose we just don't match this time around."

"It's not fair. I was all ready for a brother. We've been waiting months and months."

"There will be others, son. There are thousands of children coming over," Mr. Williams said, trying to hide his own disappointment.

"I don't know why they waited so long to start sending them," Mrs. Williams said, suddenly angry. "It'll be winter soon and that journey's hard enough in the winter, without submarines to worry about. They should have started months ago."

"Oh, Mary, we can't start worrying about that kind of thing."

Bob was stunned by the news. He had always assumed that when the British children came to Saskatoon, one of them would come to stay. Mrs. Williams had been on the committee from the first day. It did not make sense to Bob that no one was coming to his house. He could not believe it. Mrs. Williams saw how upset Bob was and gave him a hug.

"Now don't worry. Your father's right! There are thousands more still to come. We're bound to get someone soon."

"I still don't think it's fair; there's nothing wrong with our house."

"Everyone knows that, dear. But there are only thirty children and lots of volunteers. We'll just have to wait."

No more British children came to Saskatoon. School started and Bob came home every day and asked his mother when the guest child was coming. Mrs. Williams always answered that she had no news. The children who did arrive in Canada during the first weeks of September stayed in Ontario.

"They say there aren't enough coming — they don't need to send them all the way here," Mrs. Williams said one day. "The bombings are going on and they send a few hundred when they should be sending thousands. It's shameful."

One day late in September, Bob came home to find his mother looking strained, as if she had been crying.

"Oh Bob, the news is just terrible. It was on the radio. A whole shipload of children has gone down in the Atlantic. Torpedoed. How could anyone torpedo a ship carrying children? How could they?"

The story came out gradually. The *City of Benares*, carrying evacuees from Britain, had been in a convoy of ships crossing the Atlantic. Three hundred miles from Ireland, the naval escort left the convoy. There were not enough ships to escort the convoy all the way to Canada and the navy thought that there were no submarines that far out in the ocean. The navy had been wrong. The convoy sailed on, running into bad weather with high waves, rain and hail. The children went to bed each night with their clothes on, wearing lifebelts. One night at about ten o'clock, while the children were in bed, an explosion rocked the ship. A torpedo from a submarine had hit it. Some of the children, sleeping in cabins near where the torpedo hit, were killed by the explosion. The rest of the children went up on deck, into the rain and hail, to find their lifeboats. The boats were lowered, but the sea was so rough that most of them were swamped. The passengers had to sit waist deep in the icy water. Some children could not get to the boats but clung for their lives to rafts and wreckage. Twenty minutes after being hit, the *City of Benares* sank and the survivors were left in the storm to wait for rescue. The cold was so intense that the children in the boats began to die. When morning came and the rescue ships found the boats and rafts, nearly ninety children had died.

The story shocked everyone. Mr. Williams shouted about butchery. "They did the same in the last war," he said. "They don't care about women and children."

As a result of the disaster, the British government decided not to send any more children to Canada that winter. If there were enough ships in the spring of 1941, the evacuation would start again.

"So we'll have to wait 'til spring," Mr. Williams said when the news came on the radio.

"I don't think they'll start again," Mrs. Williams said sadly. "I don't believe either government ever really wanted the children to come here anyway. Not the British and not the Canadian. We forced them."

"Danny said something like that," Bob nodded.

"He said his uncle's committee tried to bring people over, but the Canadian government wouldn't let them come."

"I remember you saying that, Bob. Well, I think it's shameful. Now no one's coming. They'll all have to stay over there — right on the front line. That's no place for children."

Bob and Danny weren't so sure. As they read the paper every day and looked at the pictures of the bomb damaged cities and photos of people living in caves and underground railway stations, it all looked very exciting. Saskatoon seemed dull and far away from the action. Even though the air training school had opened, no one could pretend that Saskatoon was on the front line. After Fred was posted to Britain, Danny even talked about running away to join the air force.

"It would have been swell to have had a brother who had been in the war," Bob said to Danny one day as they cycled back from watching the planes at the airport. "I wish he had come. I bet he would have had some terrific stories."

CHAPTER 5

BOB delivered his last copy of the *Star-Phoenix* and headed home. Snow was falling heavily, blown by bitter winds. Bob's jacket and wool pants were wet and his feet were freezing. Although it was just a week into November, the city was buried under snow. People had begun to put their cars away for the winter, jacking them up on blocks and draining the water from the radiators. The streetcars that rumbled up Twelfth Street were packed with men and women on their way home from work. Through the frosted windows, Bob could barely see the dim shapes of the passengers. "At least they're warm," he thought, feeling the wind cut into his face.

Bob ran home as quickly as he could and raced up the path, bursting into the house through the back door. He dropped his bag and pulled off his scarf and jacket, stamping the snow from his boots before he kicked them off. The kitchen was bright, warm, and full of good smells. Aunt Peg was making hot chocolate and she looked up and smiled at Bob.

"Hello, Bob. I thought you'd like something warm."

"Thanks, Auntie. It's a real blizzard out there."

"No night for a sailor, as Uncle Arthur says."

The chocolate was too hot to drink, but Bob was glad to wrap his hands around the mug and feel the warmth through the thick china. Bob could hear the metronome and the piano in the living room. From time to time he heard his mother speaking quietly to her piano student. These were familiar sounds of the school year and they made Bob feel good, even though it reminded him that soon he would have to do his own practising.

"I heard from your Uncle Arthur today," Aunt Peg said as she began to peel potatoes. "He's back in an Eastern Canadian port," she laughed. That was the phrase the newspapers always used in stories. They were not allowed to publish the names of ports where ships docked. "He says he's glad to be back in Halifax. Says they ran into a couple of big storms this time, but it kept the subs quiet. He says he'd rather be bouncing around than be watching for subs in a calm sea."

"Can I see the letter, Auntie?" Bob asked eagerly.

"Well, no, Bob. It's not all about Corvettes."

Bob grinned and began to drink his chocolate. He liked Aunt Peg and it was fun to have her staying with them.

Aunt Peg had moved in with the Williamses while she was waiting to go to Halifax to be near her husband. Saskatoon was so full of war workers that it would have been impossible for her to find anywhere else to live. Bob enjoyed talking to his aunt and it was good to come home to a hot drink after his paper route. His mother was never free until her last student had gone.

"Your mum's got some special news," Aunt Peg said, lifting the pan of potatoes onto the stove.

"What is it?"

"Oh, she'll want to tell you herself. Go warm up for your practice before supper."

"You guys gang up on me all the time. I don't stand a chance."

"Well, we are sisters," Aunt Peg said. "Why don't you check the furnace? It's going to be a cold night."

Bob gulped his chocolate and grabbed a couple of cookies to take down to the basement. Stoking the furnace was one of his favourite chores. When he opened the door, the red glow of the fire filled the basement. Bob liked to imagine that he was on his uncle's Corvette, stoking the boilers and keeping up the steam as the ship ploughed through the Atlantic on its search for submarines. As Bob shovelled in the coal, the fire flared, then the glow died down as the fresh coal was piled on. Bob shut the furnace door and went upstairs to wash before practising the piano.

Mr. Williams didn't come home for supper. The blizzard had delayed the trains and the schedules were all upset, so everyone at the station had to work late. Bob helped himself to the mashed potatoes and meat loaf, covering them with half a jug of gravy.

"Auntie says you've got some special news, mum."

"Yes, I have, dear. It's very exciting, I think. Can you guess what it is?"

"Well, I know the war hasn't ended. So what is it?"

"It's very close to home," Mrs. Williams smiled.

"Oh, Mary, for goodness sake, why don't you just tell the child," Peg said. "Don't torment him!"

"Well, Bob, we had a committee meeting this afternoon — an evacuees' committee. There was a bit of a problem."

"What kind of problem, mum? There haven't been any new evacuees for months."

"No, but there was a boy staying out near Plunkett with relatives. He's had some trouble fitting in — the adults are quite old and not used to having children around the house."

"What'll happen to him, mum?" Bob asked, already guessing what she would say.

"Well," Mrs. Williams said, "he'll need a new home."

"Why do you do this, Mary," Peg said with a half laugh. "You never tell a story straight. Always spin it out and twist it around."

"I'm just telling it as I learned about it."

"Mum, come on. What's going to happen to this kid? Is he coming here? That's it, isn't it?" His voice rose with excitement.

"Yes. That's it — straight," Mrs. Williams laughed. "You'll have your brother after all. The boy's coming to town tonight, on the train from Plunkett. I said we'd take him and the committee agreed."

Bob looked at his mother and Aunt Peg. Everyone was smiling and Bob felt as if Christmas had come early.

"I think that's swell, mum. I'm glad you're on that committee. A brother!"

"Perhaps you should tell Bob a bit about him," Aunt Peg said as she cleared the dishes.

"Well, he's twelve, same as you Bob. He comes from Kent, near London, right where the bombers come over from Germany — that's why he got onto one of the first parties sent over. His father's with the British Army in Egypt — he drives a truck, or is it a tank? He's an only child. That's about all I know."

"Boy, I can't wait to ask him about the war. I mean, imagine being right there when the bombers came over. Maybe he saw Spitfires and stuff."

"Be careful about that, Bob. Some of the children don't like to talk about it if they've had a bad time. Let him get settled before you start cross examining him."

Aunt Peg served the apple pie and ice cream and poured coffee for herself and Mrs. Williams. Bob ate happily, his mind full of plans for showing off his new brother. He imagined the two of them arriving at school on Monday morning, and everyone crowding round to meet the new kid. "Yeah, this is my new brother," he would say casually.

"Mum, what's his name? You never told us his name!"

"It's David Harris."

"He will be going to Albert, won't he?"

"Oh, yes, all the guest children go to the local school."

"Swell."

"Questions, questions," Mrs. Williams laughed. "Any more?"

"Where will he sleep, mum? Auntie Peg's using the spare room."

"I know." There was a pause. "He'll have to share your room."

That was a shock. He had never thought that when his brother moved into the house he would move into Bob's room. Bob toyed with the last forkful of pie on his plate.

"My room's awfully small, mum. And there's only one bed; will you be getting another?"

"Of course not. You'll only have to share until Aunt Peg goes to Halifax. That won't be so hard."

"Two of us in one bed," Bob said doubtfully.

"For goodness sake, child, lots of children share a bed. Just think of it as doing your bit for the war effort."

"It'll be fine, Bob," Aunt Peg said. "You're good at getting on with people — you'll manage."

"Yeah, I suppose so, Auntie."

"It'll be like a sleepover," Mrs. Williams said brightly, "only you boys had better not plan on talking until midnight every night."

"Well, not every night, mum."

Bob was lying on the floor listening to the hockey

game when Mr. Williams arrived home. His father came into the living room carrying his supper on a tray and settled down in the big chair by the radio.

"Who's ahead?"

"The Leafs, dad — one up on Detroit."

"Good. This year we'll get the cup, right?"

"Hope so, dad. I couldn't take another series like last year."

The two of them had listened to the game every Saturday night for years. They both supported the Leafs and had been shattered when their team lost the Stanley Cup after three overtime defeats in the finals. Bob always sprawled on the floor, resting his chin on his hands. His feet now touched a small table near the wall that they had not reached last season and he enjoyed the feeling of being that much taller. Halfway into the second period, the doorbell rang. Mrs. Williams hurried from the kitchen to open the door. A wave of cold air rolled through the room, and Bob shivered and rose to his knees.

"Come on in. Don't stand around outside."

As Mrs. Smith came into the room, Mr. Williams stood up, and turned the radio down. He helped her take off her snow-covered coat. When Mr. Williams stepped aside, Bob suddenly saw a small boy standing a step behind Mrs. Smith. It was almost as though Mr. Williams had done a conjuring trick, producing the boy with a shake of Mrs. Smith's coat. That made Bob laugh and the boy flushed.

"Here, Bob, take David's suitcase and say hello.

David, give me that wet coat. Come on in and get warm," Mrs. Williams said, taking David's coat and scarf and half pushing him into the living room.

"Hi, David," Bob said.

"Hello," David walked slowly into the room, looking around as if he hoped to see something familiar. His hair stood up at the back of his head where he had pulled off his toque. His large ears were red with cold.

Bob went to pick up the suitcase. Strapped on the outside was a bat with a long blade, flat on one side and wedge shaped on the other. It had a long handle covered in red rubber.

"Hey, is that a cricket bat?" Bob asked.

"Of course it is," David snapped. "What does it look like?"

There was a silence; the tiny voice of Foster Hewitt crackled from the radio and the crowd cheered. Mr. Williams turned the radio off.

"Well, we don't play too much cricket around here, David, not at this time of year. It's mostly hockey."

"I don't have a hockeybat."

Bob laughed and the four adults all smiled. David turned bright red.

"I mean stick. Everyone knows it's a stick. Hockey's a stupid girls' game. Jolly hockey sticks," he shouted.

"It's okay, David," Aunt Peg said. "There's no need to get upset over a little slip of the tongue. It just sounded a bit funny to us, that's all."

David glowered for a moment, relaxed and then said, "I'm sorry. I shouldn't fly off the handle like that."

"Why is everyone standing around?" Mr. Williams said. "Mrs. Smith, sit down, and you too, Mary. I'll get you some coffee. Bob, take that case upstairs. You must be starving David. Come into the kitchen and we'll fix you some bacon and eggs."

Bob carried the case upstairs, and turned on the light in his room. It looked very small. The big bed took up a lot of space. When Bob put the suitcase down at the foot of the bed there was not much room to spare. "Well, he's here now," Bob thought and laughed to himself as he remembered the hockeybat. The picture of David all red faced and angry, flashed into his mind. Bob suddenly remembered seeing that red, flushed face once before. The ears. "I've met him!" Bob said and his heart sank as he remembered where it had been. "He's that kid at church. Oh, swell. I'm going to be locked in a tiny room with a mad elephant."

When Bob went downstairs, David was sitting in the kitchen. Mr. Williams carried a great plateful of bacon and eggs to the table and offered David a plate of bread.

"Thank you, Mr. Williams. May I please have some milk?"

"Sure, David. Bob, get David some milk."

"We met before, didn't we, David?" Bob said as he brought the pitcher to the table and poured milk for both of them. "In the summer, remember?"

"No, I'm afraid I don't. Where?"

"At church."

"I've met a lot of people since I got here," David said apologetically.

"Well, you boys will have plenty of time to get to know each other. Though I hope you won't be here too long, David."

"I'll try not to be too much trouble, Mr. Williams."

"Oh, that's not what I meant," Mr. Williams said, looking embarrassed. "I just meant I hope the war will end soon and you can get back home."

"So do I, Mr. Williams, but I'm afraid it doesn't look too good."

CHAPTER 6

"I'VE met him before, dad," Bob said.

Mrs. Williams had taken David upstairs to help him unpack and get settled. Bob and his father had caught the end of the game on the radio and were listening to a dance band while they waited for the news.

"Where would that have been, Bob?"

"You remember that Sunday at church when all the guest kids came, in the summer?"

"Sure. Did you talk to him then?"

"Well, we nearly had a fight. I mean, he said I was laughing at him and stuff like that. I wasn't, but he was mad and he made me mad, you know."

"I do," Mr. Williams laughed, "but he seems nice enough now. He was probably a bit worked up then — just got here after all, hadn't he?"

"Yeah, I suppose so," Bob said thoughtfully. "I hope this will work, dad."

"Give it a chance, Bob, and I bet it will. No reason why it shouldn't, is there?"

Bob did not answer. He lay on his back, staring up at the ceiling while the radio announcer read the news. There had been more raids on Britain and the RAF was bombing towns in Italy and Germany. It seemed that the Italian invasion of Greece was slowing down. "No blitzkrieg there," Mr. Williams said happily, "not like the Germans last spring." The big news was from Egypt where the British Army was getting ready for a major attack on the Italians.

"That's where David's dad is. I wonder if David knows what's going on there?" Bob asked, looking over at his father.

"Shouldn't think so, son. His father wouldn't be able to write much about it. You know what Uncle Arthur's letters are like."

"What about Arthur's letters?" Mrs. Williams asked as she came into the room.

"We were just talking about David's dad, being in Egypt. Bob was wondering if he'd have news from there."

"He's up there now, reading letters. He says his mother writes quite often. Do you know, Bob, Mrs. Harris numbers all her letters so David will know if any get lost? He says that two never made it here."

"What happened, mum?"

"David thinks the ships carrying them were sunk. It really brings the war home to you when you hear something like that."

"Yeah. Maybe he saw subs on the way over. I'm going to ask him. I bet he's had some real adventures."

"Just remember not to pry too much and give him a chance to bring the subject up," Mrs. Williams said.

When Bob went up to the bedroom, David was in his pyjamas, looking at the maps of the Atlantic and North Africa which Bob had pinned to the wall. Bob noticed a few new things in the room. Some books and a square cardboard box with a long string handle stood on the dresser. Alongside them, in a brass frame, was a photo of a man in army uniform. A woman stood on one side of him, David on the other. The man had his arms around them and was smiling into the camera. The woman and the boy were not smiling. In front of the picture was a silver badge of a tank. Bob picked it up. "What's in that cardboard box, David? I saw a girl with one of those at the station."

"It's a gas mask. We were supposed to leave them behind, but some of us brought them. They're awfully smelly."

David turned away from the maps. When he saw the badge in Bob's hands, he shouted, "Put that down. It's my father's, he's in the Tank Corps."

"I was just looking."

"Well, I'd rather you didn't just go picking up my things, if you don't mind. How would you like it if I just poked around in your stuff, like this?"

David snatched at a letter pinned beside the maps and tore it from the wall. He seemed about to crunch it into a ball.

"Hey, watch it," Bob yelled. "That's from the Prime Minister."

"What, from Mr. Churchill?" David sounded surprised and began to read the letter aloud.

Dear Mr. Williams,
The Prime Minister has asked me to reply to your letter on child refugees. He wishes to thank you for your concern about this question and wishes you to know that he recognizes the complexity of the situation. In these difficult times, expressions of opinion such as yours are most valuable when decisions must be made.

Yours sincerely,

Bob had never been able to read the signature. When Danny had read the letter, he had laughed and said it was the kind of thing his uncle always got from Ottawa.

"It's not signed by Churchill. Anyway, what's it all about?"

"Well, I wrote to our Prime Minister, Mr. King. I said he should let more children come to Canada to get away from the war."

"Oh, I say, how jolly decent of you. Opening your home to a poor refugee from the war. I do hope he'll be grateful," David sneered.

"Jeez, David, what's with you? No one asked you to read the letter. You asked and I told you."

They glowered at one another until David dropped the letter and pushed past Bob to get into bed. Bob picked the letter up, folded it along its creases, and put it in a drawer. "He might do something stupid to it," he thought, glaring over at David who stared at him from the bed. Bob began to undress and put on his pyjamas. It was very quiet in the room. Bob knew David was still watching him and it made him feel embarrassed, just as he felt in the cabin at camp the first couple of nights. Bob turned off the light before he put on his pyjama bottoms.

"Sure you can find the string in the dark?" David giggled.

"I'll manage, thanks," Bob said, tying the pyjama cord. He climbed into bed and pulled up the covers. Light reflected from the fresh snow outside and shone brightly around the edges of the curtain, lighting parts of the room. The two boys lay quietly, gradually relaxing as they grew drowsy.

"There's a blackout at home," David said, almost to himself. "When you put up the blinds no light comes in and, if any light shows, the Air Raid Wardens shout, 'Put that light out,' when they go by in the street. There are no lights in the street. It was wizard to see the street lights shining when we reached Quebec."

"What way did you come over, David?"

"From Liverpool. We had to sail all around the top of Ireland and then into the Atlantic. It was very rough. Why do you have a map of the Atlantic on the wall?"

"My Uncle Arthur's on Corvettes with the RCN. He's always saying how rough it is at sea."

"Yes. Most of the escorts and the children were

sick. We ran into a big storm a couple of days out. The ship was rolling around and the screws came right out of the water — it made the whole ship shake."

"Weren't you scared?"

"No. And I wasn't sick either. It was jolly interesting. We could go all over the ship. I went down to the engine room and up to the crow's nest — right at the top of the mainmast. That's where the sailors went to look for subs."

"Did you see any?"

"I saw a ship get torpedoed. It blew up and caught fire. The destroyers were sailing around looking for the U-boat and picking people out of the water."

"Can you see U-boats? I mean, aren't they too deep in the water?"

"They have to come near the surface to fire their torpedoes." David paused and seemed to think for a moment or two. "That's how I saved our ship."

"Saved your ship?"

"Yes. I was up in the crow's nest, you see, and I looked over to the starboard — that's the right — and I saw a torpedo track in the water. I yelled down to the captain to warn him and he just turned the ship in time and the torpedo missed us and went straight into another ship. And it went up — boom — and there was fire everywhere."

"Did that really happen, David?"

"Of course it did. Later on there was a big ceremony. The passengers were all there in the first class saloon. The captain made a speech and thanked me for saving all of us. He said I could go up in the crow's nest anytime I wanted, even though passengers weren't really supposed to go. Everyone clapped and the ship's orchestra played and everything."

"Ah, come on, David. You don't expect me to believe that."

"They gave me a certificate."

"Boy, I'd really like to see that."

"I lost it."

Bob began to laugh and David sat up. Bob could see the dark shape of David's head, his big ears silhouetted in the dim light. Bob began to laugh even harder.

"What's so funny?" David said in a tight, angry voice.

"You are, Dumbo. That's such a stupid story, you can't expect anyone to believe that stuff."

"You can think what you like. Actually, I don't care at all what you think."

David lay down and rolled over on his side, pulling the covers from Bob. Bob pulled them back. David twisted and turned and the bed bounced up and down. Neither of them spoke again. Bob lay wondering about what David had said. "He must think I'm really dumb telling a story like that. Lost the certificate." Bob grinned to himself in the dark and almost began to giggle, but he managed to stifle it. David snorted and kicked his feet. Bob heard Aunt Peg and his parents come up to bed before he managed to fall asleep.

David heard the adults, too, as he lay awake. The

59

house grew quiet, but David could hear all the unfamiliar little sounds of his new home. There were creaks and cracks in the woodwork, gurgling and banging in the radiators and soft sounds that he could not identify. A tree branch tapped on the wall outside. The house was hot. Every Canadian house he had been in was hot and the inside of his nose always felt dry. Sometimes his nose bled, as it had never done at home. David slipped out of bed and stood barefooted on the linoleum covered floor. Bob stirred but did not wake up. David felt his way around the bed and slowly opened the bedroom door. There was enough light to find his way to the kitchen.

David got himself a glass of water, trying not to make too much noise. A row of jars stood on the counter and David began lifting the lids quietly, poking his fingers into the jars. He felt flour and sugar, salt, and macaroni. One large jar held cookies and David took a handful, eating them greedily and scattering crumbs over the counter and the floor. He took some more, swilling them down with the water. It felt good to eat so many cookies so quickly. David began opening the cupboards, but it was too dark to see what was inside most of them. In the cupboard near the window, he could see a small jar. When he put his fingers into that, he felt cold metal coins and paper. David closed the cupboard door quietly.

The kitchen felt hot and stuffy and David tiptoed to the back door. He was surprised to find it unlocked. The snow had stopped and moonlight shone on the drifts in the back yard, making the snow sparkle. It was quiet and cold outside. David shivered and quickly shut the door. He sprang the catch and heard the lock click into place. It made him feel better, knowing the door was locked, and he picked his way on icy feet back to the staircase and the bedroom.

"Whassaassa," Bob muttered as David eased himself back into bed.

"Oh, put a sock in it," David whispered. He could see the dark shape of North Africa on the map on the wall. Somewhere down there, his father might be driving around the desert at this very moment. It was a long way away and thinking about it made David feel miles from anywhere that mattered. "Take care of yourself, dad," he thought. It was a kind of prayer he said every night before he fell asleep.

CHAPTER 7

THE smell of bacon filled the kitchen and there was a plate of pancakes warming in the oven when Bob and David came down to breakfast. "Better get to it, boys," Mrs. Williams said, "we'll have to be off to church soon."

"That bacon smells good, Mrs. Williams. Mum says they've cut the bacon ration to four ounces a week now. I wish I could send her some."

"Well, we could do that, David," Mrs. Williams said. "You can get it in cans. In fact, we could send her a food parcel — it might even get there for Christmas."

"I bet she'd be jolly pleased," David said as he sat down and helped himself to bacon and pancakes. Aunt Peg and Mrs. Williams smiled at him.

"Leave some for me, David," Bob said. He meant it to sound joking, but it came out sharper than he intended and David looked up at him with a frown. David's face cleared and he said, "It's all right, Bob. There's lots."

"There'd better be," Mr. Williams said. He shut the back door behind him and stamped snow off his boots. "I've just been doing the path. There's a lot of snow, but it's settled now." He came into the room and sat down at the table, wrapping his hands around the coffee mug. Bob passed the dishes to his father, who heaped food onto his own plate.

"Funny thing," Mr. Williams said as he cut into the pancakes, "when I went to go out this morning, the door was locked. Can't think why."

"I did it, Mr. Williams," David said. "I came down for a drink of water and the door was unlocked, so I locked it."

"Oh, we never do that, David. No one around here does."

"Aren't you afraid of burglars?"

"Why, no one worries about that, David," Aunt Peg said. "We all leave our doors open."

"You couldn't do that at home," David said. "My father always made sure the doors were locked every night before he went to bed. My mum does it now."

"Well, you'll soon get used to our ways, David," Mr. Williams smiled. "I don't believe I could find the key to that door if I had to."

"I suppose you ate the cookies, David?" Mrs. Williams asked.

"Cookies, Mrs. Williams?"

"I found crumbs everywhere this morning."

"Well, yes, I did take a biscuit," David said, smiling at Mrs. Williams.

"It was a lot more than one, David. We don't let Bob have cookies after he's brushed his teeth at night and you shouldn't either. I don't want you to go home with big holes in your teeth."

"All right, Mrs. Williams, I'll remember to leave the door open and not to take the cookies." He said the last word in a strange way. It took Bob a moment to realize that David was trying to imitate Mrs. Williams's accent. Bob could see the anger in David's eyes as the English boy stared down at his breakfast. The adults sensed it, too, and there was an awkward silence until Mr. Williams said simply, "Good. Now let's all eat. Reverend Strong will be waiting for us."

The tension eased as they finished breakfast and prepared to leave for church. The bell was ringing as they reached the church. Bob had to hurry ahead to be in time to change into his choir robes.

After the service and lunch, Mrs. Williams suggested that the boys go out. Bob was glad since Sunday afternoon at home was very quiet and the time passed slowly. David seemed reluctant to leave, but he pulled on his boots and followed Bob out of the house.

"What do you do on Sunday afternoon in Saskatoon?" David asked as they walked down the path.

"We'll go and get Danny. Then we can walk along the river. It's pretty nifty along there."

"Who's Danny?"

"He's a friend of mine — he's in the same grade at school."

"Why wasn't he in church this morning?"

"He's Jewish."

"Oh, really," David said thoughtfully.

"What does that mean?"

"Nothing. I've lots of Jewish friends. There are Jews everywhere in Britain."

"Yeah, well we don't make a big thing of it, you know. Danny's a nice guy. His brother's in the RCAF. He's flying a Spitfire in Britain right now. Danny knows a lot about planes and things."

Danny came out of his house almost as soon as they rang the bell. He was pulling on the leather flying helmet he always wore these days. It was a gift from Fred and while it was too big for him, Danny would not wear anything else. Bob was sure Danny had slept in it for the first couple of weeks after Fred left Canada.

"Hi, Danny. This is David Harris, from Britain. He's come to stay with us."

Danny smiled. "I thought they'd stopped sending people here."

"They did. I've been living near Plunkett. The people there treated me like a home boy, so CORB moved me here. I'm staying with the Williams now."

"Who's CORB?" Danny asked as the three boys crossed the street on their way to the river bank.

"The Children's Overseas Reception Board are the people who brought us over here. If you don't like your guest, you call up CORB and tell them to take him away," David said bitterly.

"Boy, I bet my mum wishes she could do that to me sometimes," Danny laughed. Then he whooped and slid down the bank, spraying snow all around him. Bob and David followed and all three of them were laughing as they reached the path. Danny led the way into the thick bushes which grew on each side of the path.

"Is that a flying helmet, Danny?" David said.

"Yeah. Nifty, isn't it. My brother gave it to me. He's flying Hurricanes with the RCAF."

"Oh, Bob said he was in Spitfires."

"Well, Bob has a job keeping them straight. He's more a navy type than air force."

"The Hurricane's a super plane. They're really wizard to watch, they climb so fast. Better than a Messerschmitt."

"Where did you see them?" Danny asked.

"We live in Kent, near London, you know, and lots of German planes came over. I saw dogfights all the time. The planes all fly around and the sky's full of vapour trails. Sometimes you can see tracer bullets glowing in the sky."

"Did you ever see anyone shot down?"

"Lots of times. One big bomber — a Dornier — crashed in a field just behind our school. In the morning when we went to school, it was still smoking. And I saw parachutes. A German pilot was caught just down the street from us. The Home

Guard marched him away. You see German prisoners all the time — at railway stations. They're always being moved around."

"Isn't it kind of scary? Air raids must be really bad," Bob said.

"No, it's exciting," David said as Bob caught up with him where the path broadened and they could walk side by side behind Danny. "Most of the time you're in an air raid shelter. We had one in our garden. You could stand at the door and watch. The bombers would come over on their way to London, the searchlights would go on and the ack-ack guns would start up. You could see the shells exploding in the sky. Then bombs would start falling and there'd be fire everywhere. And you'd see a big red glow in the sky over London from all the fires there."

"And you weren't scared?" Bob asked.

"Of course not. Why should I be scared?"

"All that bombing and stuff. Anyone would be scared."

"Are you calling me a coward?" David stopped and turned to face Bob. David's fists were clenched and he crouched at the knees, glaring up at Bob. "Do you want to try something?"

"Hey, guys, what's going on?" Danny called, turning and coming back to the two of them.

"He called me a coward," David muttered.

"Oh, keep your shirt on," Bob said disgustedly. "I never called you a coward."

"Come on, guys," Danny said. David dropped his

fists and turned away from Bob, walking along the path with Danny. "Every time you talk to the guy, he ends up boasting and then getting mad. He's really stupid," Bob thought. But David and Danny were getting along fine, chattering to each other and laughing. David was telling a story, using his two hands like planes to show Danny how a dogfight between fighter planes was fought. Danny gestured in return, telling David what Fred had said about tactics. Bob followed the two of them along the winding path on the river bank. He listened to David and Danny talking and laughing. Once, Danny turned and shouted, "Hey, come on Bob. You should hear this," but Bob hung back without answering. Not until they reached the railway embankment and struggled up the icy slope and onto the foot path at the side of the railway bridge, did Bob join the others.

"What were you doing, Bob? You missed some wizard stuff. David's seen all sorts of things in the blitz and everything. His dad was evacuated from Dunkirk and only just got away."

"Is that so?" Bob muttered. "How many medals did he win?"

"David didn't say anything about medals." Danny looked at Bob with a puzzled frown. "Are you okay, Bob? You seem angry," he added in a quieter voice.

"Yeah, I'm okay, Danny. Nothing's wrong."

The three boys walked to the centre of the bridge and stopped there. Behind them, they could hear the drone of the planes from the training school, flying circuits around the airport.

"I always expect to hear sirens when I hear planes," David said, turning his head to watch the planes. "That's an Anson, isn't it?"

"Yeah, and they've got Harvards too," Danny said. "Of course it's not as exciting as Spitfires and Hurricanes."

"No, it's not, really," David said as he turned back to look at the town. "And that's not like London. Still, I suppose it is bigger than Plunkett. Have you ever been there, Danny? Two elevators and a railway station — that's it."

"No," Danny laughed. "Maybe I blinked when we were passing through. Anyway, Saskatoon's not so bad. There are all kinds of things to do, and nearly fifty thousand people living here."

"Just wait till spring," Bob said, staring down at the ice on the river. "The ice gets thicker and thicker all winter. Then when spring comes, it starts to break up. It makes a noise like explosions and then it begins to move. It's really something. Everyone comes down to the river to watch it going over the dam."

"My, that sounds thrilling," David said sarcastically. "Do all fifty thousand people come? What do they do the rest of the year while they're waiting for the ice to melt?"

That made Bob mad. He grabbed David's sleeve and pulled him around so that the two of them stood face to face.

"You think you're pretty smart, don't you?"

David swung at Bob and hit him on the ear with his fist. Bob's ear stung. He grabbed David and began to wrestle with him. David was wiry, but he could not stop Bob from wrestling him to the ground. Bob knelt on David's shoulders and was going to punch him when Danny grabbed him from behind.

"Hey, cut it out. Get off him, Bob." Danny pulled at Bob and dragged him to his feet. "What's with you guys, anyway?" Danny reached down and gave David a hand. David glared at Bob and there were tears in his eyes.

"I slipped," David said. "You won't get me that easily next time."

"I could finish you off with one hand behind my back anytime," Bob sneered.

"Well, you are twice his size — one hand'd be fair," Danny said. Bob looked down at the slight English boy standing there covered in snow, his clothes twisted around his thin body. Bob felt almost ashamed. The anger drained out of him and he looked at Danny and said, "Yeah, I guess you've got a point there, Danny."

"Half-pint Harris, is that what we should call you, David?" Danny said.

"I'd rather you didn't." David replied so seriously that Bob and Danny both laughed. David smiled slightly.

The bridge started to shake under them. Looking

toward the city, they could see a train moving onto the bridge. The locomotive was sending great clouds of smoke and steam into the air. Steam hissed from between the wheels. Suddenly the walkway seemed too narrow to let the train go by without hitting them. High above their heads, the driver leaned from his cab. Bob and Danny waved to him and he waved back. As the locomotive began to pass, they were lost in a cloud of smoke and steam and the driver blew his whistle.

"Isn't it great?" Danny shouted.

The smoke cleared. Bob turned and saw David running as fast as he could along the walkway. At the end of the bridge he jumped onto the embankment and slid down the icy slope, landing in a heap on the snow at the bottom. David was still lying there when the other boys reached him. They helped him up and brushed the snow off him.

"I'm not scared of engines," he said. He shook them off and walked away along the path.

Danny and Bob watched David as he hurried along the path ahead of them.

"What are you so angry about, Bob?" Danny said.

"What do you mean?"

"I don't know. You just seem mad."

"Why don't you ask him? He's always boasting and telling lies. He's a jerk."

"He seems okay to me, Bob. And he does have some wizard stories."

"Wizard!" Bob kicked at the snow and sent a shower flying. "And why did he run away from the train like that?"

"Who knows? Hey, come on, he's waiting — he looks a bit lost."

"Oh swell, a brother who's too dumb to find his way home," Bob said to himself as he hurried after Danny.

CHAPTER 8

"NOW, David, you must write home tonight," Mrs. Williams said after supper.

"I'll do it later, Mrs. Williams."

"Now, David, I think you should write home every Sunday. You have to keep in touch."

Mrs. Williams brought paper to the table and David had to sit down and write. Bob went to the workshop in the basement and joined his father. Bob was making a fretwork sewing basket for his mother. He had begun it months before, but now he was worried about getting it finished for Christmas. He concentrated on following the pattern with his saw, trying not to hurry and spoil the work. The workshop was quiet for a long time as the two of them worked. They could hear the murmur of voices from the kitchen.

"David seems to be settling in well," Mr. Williams said.

"He's okay, I guess."

"You don't sound too enthusiastic, Bob."

"Nah, he's okay."

Mr. Williams put down his chisel and looked at Bob.

"What's the problem? Are you boys having trouble?"

"I'm not sure, dad. He's so snappy. Half the time he's boasting about what he's done, but if you call him on it, he gets mad and tries to start a fight. He just acts like a jerk."

"He seems polite enough to the rest of us. You aren't teasing him or anything are you, Bob?"

"No, dad. He's the one who starts everything."

"Well, give him a chance, son. He'll need a bit of time to settle in."

"Just so he doesn't throw his weight around all the time."

"Bob, come on up now. School tomorrow," Mrs. Williams called. Bob put away his tools and went upstairs. David was addressing an envelope. His letter lay on the table, along with two tea bags.

"What're the tea bags for, David?"

"I'm sending them to my mother. I think she'll be jolly interested. We don't have tea bags at home. I think she'll get a good laugh from them."

"Yeah, I guess they are a bit odd."

"Come on, boys. It's time for bed now," said Mrs. Williams.

Upstairs, they both felt a bit awkward changing with someone else in the room. Then David got his foot stuck in his pyjama leg and began to hop around the room until he lost his balance and fell over the bed. They both began to laugh.

"You looked like this guy at camp," Bob said to David. "We sewed his pyjama leg shut and he got so mad. He hopped around the cabin and yelled at us."

"We did that at Cub camp last summer at Skegness. There was this boy who was always crying. He was an absolute weed. Anyway, he got so angry at us that Akela had to move him to another tent. And then he went home."

"Do you go camping often?" Bob asked.

"Only with the Cubs."

"We've got a Scout troop at St. James. You could join, and then if you're still here next summer, you could come to camp with us."

"I don't think I'll be here next summer."

"Will the war be over then? Danny says it'll go on for years if the Germans don't invade Britain this summer."

"Yes, I expect he's right."

"Then why won't you be here? They won't let you go home before the war's over."

"No, they won't. But I've been moved once so I'll probably be moved again."

"My mum wouldn't do that."

"We'll see, shan't we" David said, rolling over on his side. He lay awake for a long time after Bob had fallen asleep. David heard the adults coming up to bed; then the house was quiet. Still, he could not sleep. He slipped out of bed and felt his way out of the room. Downstairs, he opened the refrigerator and began to eat ice cream from the container. "It's jolly good," he thought. He only had ice cream a couple of times a year at home. On the ship, all the children had gorged on ice cream. David ate it every chance he had after that. David put the container back in the freezer and carefully washed the spoon and put it away. Then he took a handful of cookies from the jar and ate them as he wandered around the house.

The house was quiet, creaking a little, the hot water in the radiators sometimes gurgling. None of the sounds were like those he heard in his own home back in Kent. That house was built of brick and had no central heating. David went to the back door and opened it to look out on the yard. "It's so white," he thought. "I bet there are still flowers in the garden at home." In the distance, David could hear the planes droning around the airport. He shut the door quietly and locked it before going up to bed. Then he fell asleep.

David dreamed of the seaside. He was walking along the promenade with his father and mother, eating an ice cream cone. Toby, David's dog, was jumping around his feet, begging for ice cream. David gave the rest of his cone to Toby and then they were running on the beach together down to the sea. Toby ran into the water and David followed him. The waves slapped at his legs and then a big one broke over him, drenching him to the waist and soaking his cotton summer shorts. The water felt curiously warm and his shorts clung to him as he struggled back to the beach.

David stirred and woke. His pyjama trousers were wet and warm and stuck to his legs.

"Oh, crikey," David said. "What will Mrs. Williams say?"

He had not wet the bed at home since he was about three. In Canada, it had happened often. Mrs. Grey, at Plunkett, had been very angry and called him a dirty little boy. Now it had happened again.

"Jeez, David, wake up." It was Bob, poking him, "You've wet the bed."

"I didn't," David said.

"What do you mean?" Bob said as he got out of bed and turned on the light. "Get up. Help me get the sheets off."

David climbed out of bed and the two boys pulled off the wet sheet.

"It's two o'clock in the morning. What are you boys doing?" Mrs. Williams whispered as she came into the room. "I hope you don't wake your father."

"He wet the bed, mum."

"It wasn't me, it was you."

"Just look at yourself, jerk."

"Robert! You don't have to talk like that. David, get some clean pyjamas out of the drawer and go change. Bob, help me with the bed."

Bob went to the linen closet on the landing and took the clean sheets back to his room. He helped his mother remake the bed.

"It's a bit damp, but it'll do," Mrs. Williams said.

"Really swell, mum — how many times is he going to do this?"

"How do I know, Bob? We can always wash the sheets. And I'm sure David didn't want to do it. He just needs a chance to get settled."

"Talking about the CORB boy, are we?" David asked as he came back into the room.

"Off you go, Bob. Get cleaned up."

"Tell your son to grow up. I don't want him weeing over me like a dog on a gatepost."

"David, that's quite enough. I don't like that kind of talk from either of you. You can both grow up a bit," Mrs. Williams said, holding up the blankets so David could get into bed. "Now you get back to sleep, David. It's school tomorrow."

"You can send me back if you want to. I don't care."

"Don't be silly, David. Why would I send you back?" She bent down and gave him a quick kiss on the forehead. David blushed and turned his head. Mrs. Williams smiled and brushed the hair off his forehead. Bob came back into the room and Mrs. Williams waited until he got into bed before turning out the light.

"Good night, boys. Sleep well."

"Night, mum."

"Good night, Mrs. Williams," David said. When Mrs. Williams left the room, David whispered, "Now try to control yourself, Bobbie. I don't like sleeping in a puddle."

"Who do you think you're fooling, jerk? One more crack like that and you'll be getting out of bed to look for your teeth."

"Well, you won't have to look for yours. You'll find them pushed down your throat."

"Got a big friend, have you?" Bob said turning his back and pulling the covers up to his ears.

CHAPTER 9

"YOU look tired, dear," Aunt Peg said when Bob came down to breakfast next morning.

"Yeah, it wasn't a great night."

"I heard you had a bit of trouble. But just hang on. You'll have your own room again soon. That'll make things easier."

"Have you found somewhere to park me?" David asked. He stood at the kitchen door and scowled at them. Aunt Peg laughed.

"Come on in and sit down, David. You need something hot before school." She ladled hot cereal into his bowl. "You shouldn't jump to conclusions. I'm the one who's leaving — I'm going to Halifax. Then you'll have a room of your own."

"And a bed," Bob grinned.

"Yes, I'd like that," David said, "I'm not used to sleeping under water."

"Can't think why not."

They ate their breakfast in silence while Aunt Peg drank a cup of tea and watched them. She seemed to be trying to think of something to say. Then she gave a slight shrug of her shoulder and, half smiling to herself, said, "Well, don't lose David on the way to school, Bob. They're expecting him."

The boys walked up Clarence Avenue toward the big, old school. Albert School had a high tower in the centre, cement turrets around the top, and steps at each end leading up to the first floor.

"You'll like Albert. It's a swell school. We think it looks like a castle," said Bob, pointing to the school.

"Call that a castle? It looks more like a railway station."

"I only said it looked like a castle. I didn't say it was one."

"If you want to see a castle, you should see the Tower of London. It's got dungeons and everything. It really looks like a castle."

"Ah, forget it," Bob said. He looked at David, trudging along with his hands thrust deep into his overcoat pockets and a sneer on his face.

"What a load of laughs he is," Bob thought. He stopped at the store across from the school and David followed him inside. The store was long and narrow. The shelves, behind a long counter, reached up to the ceiling. At the far end of the store, under the bright lights of the meat counter, the butcher was sharpening a knife on a steel.

"Hi, Mr. Timmins," Bob greeted the store owner. "This is David Harris. He's from England. He's come to stay with us until the war's over."

"Well now. Your mother said you were getting a guest child. How are you liking it, David?"

"It's all right, thank you."

"I expect you're a bit homesick. It's a long way from home."

"Oh, no, I never get homesick or anything."

"Well, let's see what we've got." Mr. Timmins reached into the counter and brought out a chocolate bar. "There you are, David."

"I'm sorry, I don't have any money."

"This one's on me. Sort of a welcome to Saskatoon."

"Oh, that's jolly decent of you, Mr. Timmins. Thank you very much," David said as he left the store.

Bob picked a pencil from the card on the counter and paid Mr. Timmins.

"David seems like a nice young fella," Mr. Timmins said.

"Yeah. That's how he seems, all right. 'Bye Mr. Timmins."

Outside, David had unwrapped the candy bar and was stuffing chocolate into his mouth as quickly as he could. He finished the last piece just as Bob caught up with him. The air smelled of chocolate and Bob could almost taste it. David licked the last crumbs from the wrapper as they crossed the street to the schoolyard, then crumpled the wrapper and dropped it on the ground.

"You can save the foil for salvage," Bob said. "We're collecting it in school. How did you like the chocolate?"

"Not as good as English chocolate."

"How would I know, pig?"

"It was my bar, Bobbie."

"You can cut out that Bobbie stuff," Bob said angrily.

Danny saw them and came running over. He was wearing his flying helmet and breeks that buttoned over long argyle socks. Bob hated breeks and refused to wear them, but lots of the boys wore them in the winter.

"Hi, David. You decided to come to school?" Danny said.

"Hello, Danny. You planning to go golfing?" David pointed at the breeks. "You look just like my dad's boss on Saturday morning."

"Think you're pretty funny, don't you?" Danny laughed, giving David a light push. They began to wrestle, staggering around the yard, yelling and shouting while a crowd watched the mock fight and laughed at them. Danny tripped and fell into the snow and David helped him up.

"This is David Harris," Danny said to the crowd. "He's from England. He saw the Battle of Britain and everything." Some of the children nodded and said hello and Bob drifted over to join the group. He was surprised to find he felt annoyed at Danny for making the introductions.

"He's staying with us," Bob said. "He arrived on Saturday. He's been in Canada a couple of months."

"Thanks awfully, Bobbie," David said, "I don't

suppose I could have told them any of that."

"Bobbie," one of the girls giggled. Bob blushed bright red.

"Do you play hockey?" Bill Kindrachuk asked.

"Oh, no," Bob shouted, "he can't do that. He didn't bring his hockeybat."

"His what?"

"His hockeybat. That's what he calls it. But he says hockey's just a girl's game. He'd rather play cricket."

The boys in the crowd began to laugh and jeer at David. David's face went rigid with anger. "So I don't play stupid hockey. But at least I don't pee in the bed like Bobbie, like some little baby."

"That's not true."

"Yes it is. His mother's going to buy him a rubber sheet."

"You're a liar."

"Be careful if you sit next to him. You might get splashed." David grinned.

Some of the kids in the crowd were giggling and laughing, but others just looked bewildered or embarrassed. Bob was furious. He started toward David, longing to punch him and knock the grin off his face. David saw him coming and clenched his fists, ready to take him on. Danny grabbed hold of Bob and wrestled with him.

"Hey, cut it out, Bob. Take it easy. Don't mind him."

"Let go, Danny. He's asking for it and now he'll get it."

"Bob, Miss Nelson's watching. You don't want to end up in the principal's office. Just take it easy."

Some of the other boys held David, and between them they managed to keep the two of them from fighting. Just then, the bell rang and the children began to straggle toward the school.

"Come on, Hockeybat. I'll show you the way to the principal's office," Jim Hughes said, holding David by the arm.

"No one knows the way better than Jim."

"Yeah, come on, Hockeybat. You don't want a late on your first day."

David let Jim and Bill lead him toward the boys' entrance. Bob and Danny followed the crowd.

"What's going on now?" Danny asked.

"Well, you know what he was like yesterday. And last night he wet the bed and he's been saying I did it. He's really asking for it. Everybody keeps telling me he needs time to settle in. What am I supposed to do while he's doing that? Why'd they let him come here? I bet there are thousands better than him that can't get in."

"Maybe, but he's not keeping anyone out."

"I think it stinks. He's here, but your cousins aren't."

"We'll just keep trying, I guess," Danny said as they went down the steps into the mudroom.

Every morning all the children gathered in the auditorium. They sang "God Save the King" and then one of the grade eight students marched onto the stage with the Union Jack. A girl from grade eight saluted and led the school in the pledge to the flag. After the principal made a few announcements and urged them to remember the salvage drive, they all filed out to their classrooms. Bob saw David waiting outside the principal's office.

When David saw Bob and Danny at recess, he said, "They'll probably put me up a grade. This grade six work is rather easy."

"If your brain's as big as your head, they'll send you over to the varsity," Bob mumbled.

David just smiled and wandered off to watch the boys playing shinny on the rink. One of the boys called, "Come on, Hockeybat. We'll show you what kind of a game this is."

"Here's your bat — don't bust it. It's my brother's."

David stepped onto the ice and took the stick. He caught onto the game quickly and seemed to understand the instructions the boys shouted at him. He could not get the hang of shooting, but he did kick the puck into the goal once and the boys applauded that.

"Hockeybat's okay," Bill Kindrachuk said to Bob as he passed him on the ice.

"Yeah. People keep telling me that."

The boys came off the ice when the bell rang and they moved toward the school, pushing and jostling. Greg Rogers was waiting by the door and he grabbed David by the arm.

"Who's the new kid?"

"David. He's from England," one of the boys said.

"A vaccie, eh? Can't he speak for himself? How do you like it here, vaccie?"

"They don't call us evacuees," David said quietly, "they call us guest children."

Greg dropped David's arm and laughed in his face.

"Know what I call you? I call you a bomb dodger, that's what, a little coward bomb dodger."

David jumped at Greg and punched him in the stomach. It did not make much impression through the coat Greg was wearing. Greg grabbed David by the shoulders. He threw David to the ground and sat on his chest, then began tapping him lightly on each cheek.

"Don't do that again, vaccie, see? You're dumb but you're still alive, right? You won't be if you make me mad, got it?"

He gave David a stinging slap on each cheek, then got up and walked into the school. A couple of boys helped David to his feet. He rubbed his cheeks and tried not to cry.

"That was Greg Rogers. You want to keep out of his way," Bill Kindrachuk said. "He's mean."

"I rather got that impression," David said as the boys led him into school.

Bob looked at Danny who grinned back at him.

"At least you know he'll pick a fight with anyone," Danny laughed.

"Hockeybat's crazy — fighting with Greg Rogers!" Jim Hughes said. "Didn't you guys warn him about Greg?"

CHAPTER 10

AFTER school the boys walked home together. They didn't seem to have too much to say to each other. Bob went to deliver the papers; David hurried into the house where Aunt Peg was preparing supper. The piano was being played in the front room.

"Any letters for me?"

"No, dear. I expect it'll be a while before any come here for you."

"It's been ages since I got one. Dad writes as often as he can and mum writes every week. What if..."

"Now you mustn't worry yourself." Aunt Peg dried her hands and sat down at the table with David. "I know what it's like to wait for letters. Sometimes I get a whole packet at once from Arthur. One time he'd been to England and back twice before I heard from him."

"It's easy to say don't worry."

"I've told myself that often enough, too." Aunt Peg paused and twisted an empty glass between her hands. "But I've told myself that if something really bad happens they tell you soon enough. When that telegram comes, then you know it's something bad."

"What telegram?"

"Oh, you know, if Arthur's hurt or something, the navy sends me a telegram. If I haven't had that, I just try to tell myself he's all right. It's not much comfort, I know, but I'm sure you'd learn soon enough if something's wrong. If you hear nothing, well, just think everything's okay. No news is good news, you know."

"That's what my mum says. You're a lot like my mum."

Aunt Peg smiled and went back to making the supper. David sat and watched her working and humming to herself. "She is like mum," he thought, looking around the warm, brightly lit kitchen with its black and white checked linoleum and rows of glass-fronted cupboards. The kitchen here wasn't like the one at home, where, as a little boy, he used to sit and watch his mother. That kitchen had a tiled floor and a stone sink with one cold water tap which meant that Mrs. Harris always had to keep a kettle boiling on the fire for hot water. Suddenly, David felt miserable enough to cry and he looked away when Mrs. Williams came hurrying into the kitchen.

"Oh, good heavens, is that the time? I had no idea. Mr. Williams will be back soon," she said as she went over to help Aunt Peg. "Would you like to clear the table and set it, David?"

"Not really, Mrs. Williams."

"I beg your pardon?"

"I wouldn't like to set the table, Mrs. Williams."

"Well, do it anyway, David," Mrs. Williams said firmly.

"Why should I?" David snapped. "I'm not your servant. I don't have to earn my keep around here."

There was a silence in the kitchen as the two women stared at David.

"No one's talking about servants, David. Everyone helps in this family. You can see Peg making the supper and no one calls her a servant."

"But I'm not in the family, am I?"

"What do you mean, David?"

David jumped to his feet, red faced and hostile.

"I'm not in the family. I'm just someone you've taken in. I'm a guest. You can't make me work around here. I'm not a home boy. I'm not someone you took in to do odd jobs and if you don't like that, you can call up CORB and have me sent away, can't you?"

David ran out of the kitchen and up the stairs. The bedroom door slammed shut just as Bob came in from his paper route. He blew on his hands and looked at the two women standing and looking at each other.

"Did I miss something?"

"No," Mrs. Williams said distractedly. "Just set the table, would you? I have to have a few words with David."

"Ah, mum, I just got in."

"Do it, Robert."

Mrs. Williams went upstairs. They heard her knock and go into the bedroom. Bob began to set the table, banging the silverware around to show them he was annoyed. When he calmed down he asked, "So, what happened, Aunt Peg?"

"David got angry about doing chores. He seems to think he doesn't have to do anything because he's a guest child."

"Why don't we get Mrs. Smith to take him away? What good is he?"

"Who expects him to be good for anything? He's just a worried little boy."

"You know what he did? He told everyone I wet the bed."

Aunt Peg laughed and Bob looked hurt.

"Oh, Bob, you must admit it's pretty cheeky. And you didn't, so you've got nothing to worry about, have you?"

"I suppose not," Bob grinned slowly. "It did make me feel stupid when he said that in front of everyone."

"Well, now you know how he must feel."

"Yeah, when you think about it, I guess that's right."

David was the last person to sit down for supper. He looked sulky, but no one said anything. Mr. Williams began talking about the news in the papers.

"Did you see the story about Coventry? Those Germans are ruthless," he said, pointing to the newspaper story of a big air raid in Britain.

"It says that seventy-five per cent of the houses there were damaged during the raid," Aunt Peg said. "It's hard to imagine what that must be like, three blocks out of every four damaged."

"And the cathedral burnt down," Mrs. Williams added. "They're just trying to scare people out of the war."

"Your mother must be glad you're safe over here, David," Mr. Williams said.

"Yes. She must be really pleased to have a bomb dodger for a son."

"Who called you that?"

"It was Greg Rogers, dad. You know, the grade seven bully," Bob said.

"Him! You just ignore him, David. People can fight better if they don't have to worry about their children; you're helping just by being out of their way."

"Dad," Bob said, "this raid on Coventry — it's really bad, right?"

"You bet it is, Bob, bombing people's houses — women and children right in the front line. It was the same in Spain before the war began."

"Well, if it's so bad, why are we doing it?"

Everyone looked at Bob and he could see four puzzled faces staring at him from around the table.

"What do you mean, son?"

"Well, remember, a couple of weeks ago, there were pictures of Berlin in the paper. We bombed

Berlin and the paper said that happened because the Germans had bombed London first."

"Yes, that's right. I remember."

"So, why is it bad for the Germans to bomb Coventry when we bomb Berlin — there must be women and children in Berlin."

"That's stupid," David said angrily. "We only bomb factories and railways and things."

"Can they do that? Can they pick targets like that?" Bob asked.

" 'Course they can. The RAF are great. They don't bomb cathedrals and things," David sneered.

"Well, the picture in the paper showed houses blown up. And there was a story from an American in Berlin about it and he said the houses were blown up, too."

"I don't care," David said. "The Germans came over and bombed London so they deserve to get bombed. You've never been in an air raid. You don't know what it's like. People get hurt, you know."

"But sometimes you do wonder where it's all going to end," Mrs. Williams said as she gathered up the plates. "Airplanes are bombing whole cities. First the Zeppelins — remember them — then Spain, and now we're doing it, too. I can't answer your question; honestly, I can't, Bob."

"War's war," Mr. Williams said.

"But if we fight it like they do, where will it end?" Aunt Peg sounded troubled.

"I just hope it ends quickly, so I can go home."

"So do I," Bob said.

"Okay, boys. Get the dishes done now," Mr. Williams said.

David didn't move from his place when Bob got up and began scraping the dishes. Mrs. Williams watched David and, after staring at her for a long time, David slowly stood up.

"I'll dry," he said.

David was lying in bed reading his collection of letters when Bob came up to the room. David folded the letters and pushed them back into their envelopes.

"Don't mess about with these letters; they're private."

"I don't care about your letters. Who cares what your parents write to you."

The two boys lay together in the dark. Bob began to get drowsy and was just dropping off to sleep when he heard crunching sounds from David's side of the bed.

"What are you doing?"

"Nothing to do with you."

"You're eating cookies, aren't you? You know mum doesn't want us to eat cookies now."

"She's not my mum. She told me off about crumbs in the kitchen, so I thought I'd save her the worry."

"You're a total jerk."

"Steady on, Bobbie old chap. Keep your hair on."

Bob lay awake for a long time. David fell asleep and Bob listened to the sound of his breathing. He tried to imagine what it would have been like to have had a brother for years. Maybe it would have been easier than it seemed to be now. "But what if I'd had a brother like this for years? At least he'll be gone when the war's over." Bob drifted off to sleep. About two o'clock in the morning, he woke up. His leg felt wet and cold.

"Oh, jeez, not again."

Bob kicked David to wake him.

"You've done it again. You've wet the bed. Let's try and change it without waking mum," Bob whispered.

The boys got out of bed and stripped off the sheets in the dark.

"Put them in the bathroom," Bob ordered.

"Why should I? You do it."

"You messed them. Why should I take your stinking sheets to the laundry?"

David dropped them on the floor. Bob grabbed the sheets and pushed them at David, trying to rub the wet parts into David's face. David dodged, and grabbed Bob.

"I'm going to push these sheets down your throat."

"And I'm going to rub your face in it. That's how we taught Toby not to mess on the carpet," David said.

"Try it, you liar."

The light went on as Mrs. Williams burst into the room.

"Stop it at once," she ordered in a fierce, low voice. "Don't you know what time it is?"

The boys stopped struggling and knelt on the floor

glaring at each other over the tangled sheets.

"David, take those sheets to the laundry and get cleaned up. Bob, get the clean sheets. I want you both back in bed in five minutes."

"Why..." David began.

"Five minutes, now move!"

CHAPTER 11

DAVID was sitting in the kitchen when Bob came in. David had refused to help Bob with his paper route after school. "Why should I? Only poor children deliver papers. I'm not poor," he had said, going into the warm house and leaving Bob alone in the cold. Now David looked up and said eagerly, "Can I see the paper?"

"You could have seen it an hour ago," Bob said throwing it onto the kitchen table. He went to the stove to pour himself a cup of hot chocolate.

"It says that any day now the British army is going to fight the Italians in Africa," Bob said. "Isn't your dad in Africa?"

"Yes, he's with the tank corps in Egypt."

"Does that mean he'll be in those battles?"

"I expect so. Maybe he'll win a medal or something."

"If he doesn't get killed first."

As soon as the words were out of his mouth, Bob wished he could call them back. He blushed and tried to think of something to say, but his mind was blank. David looked up from the paper, his face white and his eyes shining with tears. His big teeth were bared as he hissed, "I think you stink."

"I'm sorry, David, I didn't mean to say that, scout's honour."

"Why don't you just shut up. I know what you're thinking," David's voice trembled and he jumped up from the table, grabbed the newspaper and ran upstairs. Bob sat at the table, staring at his chocolate. Then he went to practise. Aunt Peg was sitting in the big chair by the radio, knitting. She turned off the radio when Bob came in and smiled at him.

"Going to work on the Mendelsohn? That's a nice piece; it'll be very good for the Christmas concert."

"Yeah, I guess so."

Aunt Peg looked a little surprised at his glum tone, but she said nothing more as he sat down and began some scales and exercises. As he worked through the familiar pieces, Bob thought about what he had said to David.

"Every day there's a story about someone from Saskatchewan who's been killed or wounded. We all worry about Uncle Arthur — and Fred in his Hurricane or whatever. It's scary when you think about it. But it came out so dumb, like I wanted his dad to get killed. Of course I don't want that to happen. But it would serve him right if it did."

The thought just popped into his head from nowhere and it surprised and upset him. "I don't mean that!" Bob stopped playing. He felt too miserable and confused to go on. Aunt Peg looked up from her knitting.

"What's the matter, Bob? Something must be on your mind, the way you've been playing. Good thing your mother's at one of her meetings," she smiled.

"Oh, Auntie Peg."

He went over and sat on the floor, resting his back on the side of Peg's chair. He picked up a ball of khaki wool from the basket and juggled it in his hands as he spoke.

"I said something mean to David. We were talking about the war in Africa and I made some crack about his dad getting killed."

The needles stopped clicking and Aunt Peg asked, "Was he very upset?"

"Yeah, he went up to our room. I think he was going to cry."

"When he calms down, you'll be able to apologize to him. You can tell him how much you worry about Uncle Arthur. Show him you understand how he feels."

"I could try. You know something scary, Auntie?"

"What's that?"

"Just now, when I was thinking about what I'd said, I thought it'd serve him right if it happened. I mean, why did I think that?"

Aunt Peg reached down to touch Bob's hair. For a few moments she said nothing. Then she began to knit again.

"I can remember when your mum and I were little girls, we were always fighting."

"What, you two?"

"Oh, yes, even us. And they were nasty ones, too. Really vicious. There were times when we hated each other."

"Why? What did mum do to you?"

"Nothing. We just got on each other's nerves. I used to tell her I wished she was dead, and I thought I meant it. I would imagine being an only child, living like a princess in a palace."

"Did you really fight about nothing?"

"Nothing you could put your finger on. It's not easy sharing things with people — even a sister. She always gets the bigger piece of pie. You and David are alike, you know."

"Gee, I hope not, Auntie."

"Think about it. You're both only children. You've had a fine old time for twelve years and now you've got a brother — just like that. It's bound to be hard — for both of you."

"Yeah. Well, he sure seems to want trouble."

"Perhaps that's only how it seems. But you're playing on home ice, remember. He's done a lot of travelling in the last few months."

"Home ice," Bob laughed.

"Oh, I listen to the radio, too."

"I don't want his dad to get killed."

"Of course you don't. When we're mad we say lots of things we don't mean. You can always apologize to David — sticks and stones, you know."

"Yeah, well, I'll try."

There was no chance to apologize that evening. Bob could not just blurt it out when David came down to supper, not in front of the whole family. David was sulky, but no one commented on it and supper passed quietly. Afterwards, Bob went down to the workshop and spent a long time finishing the top of his mother's sewing box. The work relaxed him and Bob was very pleased when he was finished. It suddenly seemed possible that the present would be ready for Christmas. Bob was in a good mood as he stoked the furnace and watched the flames dance over the coals. The red glow lit the sheets hanging in the basement to dry. Bob banked the fire for the night and closed the furnace door. Then he put out the basement lights and quietly climbed the stairs.

The kitchen was dark when Bob opened the basement door, but he could see David standing at the counter. The cupboard by the window was open, but as soon as David heard the basement door open, he shut the door and spun around.

"Oh, it's you," David said.

"Yeah. What're you doing, David?"

"Nothing, just getting a drink of water."

"Shouldn't think you'd need that, or are you planning to float us down to Prince Albert tonight?"

"Why don't you dry up," David snarled. "Dry up," he laughed, "that's pretty funny."

Bob was so mad that he leapt across the kitchen, grabbed David and twisted his arm. The two boys started to wrestle and were soon on the floor, trying to keep quiet and to hurt each other as much as they could at the same time. David even managed to bite Bob and he caught one of Bob's fingers and bent it back sharply. Bob gave a muffled shout. The boys rolled into the table. The table scraped across the floor and one of the chairs crashed over. Seconds later the kitchen light went on.

"What's going on here? I thought someone was breaking into the house," Mrs. Williams said, glaring down at them.

"He started it, mum."

"He just jumped me for nothing."

"Big mouth."

"Bob, stop that. Get up, both of you, and tidy up this kitchen."

The boys got up and did as they were told, looking at one another angrily whenever their eyes met. Then Mrs. Williams told David to go to bed.

"Really, Bob," she said when David had gone, "what were you thinking of, fighting in the house! I don't want you two fighting anywhere, but especially not in the house."

"He started it, mum. Making wise cracks, he thinks he's so funny."

"It takes two to fight. You'll just have to show some restraint. Give him a chance, Bob."

"Why am I always to blame? He's the big mouth, he's the one who..."

"That's enough, Bob. Just try to remember he's a long way from home."

"Oh, sure."

"Don't be rude, Bob. Just get on up to bed now and remember what I've said."

Bob went upstairs, relieved to find David pretending to be asleep. Neither of them wanted to talk and Bob quickly changed and put out the light.

"Guess I won't apologize tonight," Bob muttered to himself.

CHAPTER 12

DAVID did go into grade seven, which made Bob happy. It meant that for a part of each day he was free of David.

After school while Bob was delivering the papers, David would stop for a cola at Mr. Timmins' store with some of the boys from his class. David loved cola which he had never had in Britain, and he often bought them for the other boys. He usually had to buy one for Greg Rogers, too, who had a habit of hanging around outside the store and getting younger boys to buy him things.

"Does he buy a lot of stuff at Mr. Timmins' store?" Bob asked Danny one day as they hurried to finish the papers. It was very cold outside and Bob appreciated Danny's offer of help.

"I guess so. You know, he buys the guys colas and candy bars — they're a nickel each."

"Sounds like a lot of money. I guess that's why he says he's not poor enough to deliver papers."

"Did he say that?" Danny laughed. "He sure likes to needle you, doesn't he Bob? We get on okay."

"How do you manage that?"

"Oh," Danny said quietly, "we're a bit alike."

"You and him? That's a laugh."

"Yeah, well we talk a lot when he comes over."

"Does he tell you what a big hero he is?"

"No. He's okay, Bob."

"So, what do you guys talk about?"

"Aw, you know, everything — the war, planes, and stuff. He's seen all kinds of things. You should ask him about it."

"Sure."

"In his school, there were a couple of boys — refugees from Austria — and he was friendly with them. He says he knows now what they felt like."

"You sound like you really like the guy."

"Well, we're sort of like each other," Danny said quietly.

"You already said that, but I don't get it. He acts like such a jerk."

"We both feel like outsiders sometimes." Danny tugged at the strap on his leather helmet. The boys stopped at the corner and Bob looked at his friend.

"You and him? You really feel the same?"

"I guess so. A bit anyway."

"Maybe I should ask my mum to send him to stay with you. I could come and visit him whenever I wanted to."

"Sure, and then I wouldn't see you until the war is over," Danny laughed as he turned down Clarence

Avenue toward home. Bob walked along Thirteenth Street thinking about what Danny had said. Danny and David were really hitting it off and the thought made Bob feel the same as he had on David's first morning at school. "He's supposed to be my brother," Bob said as he turned in at the gate.

David really wanted skates. He hinted about it a few times, then came right out one supper time and said, "I need skates, Mrs. Williams."

"Well, I think we might have an old pair of Bob's that would fit."

"I'm getting the hang of hockey now, but I'll have to learn to skate, won't I, if I'm ever going to play?"

The skates in the house didn't fit David, so Mrs. Williams took both boys downtown on Saturday to get them fitted with new skates. Shivering in the blustery wind, the three of them waited for the streetcar. When Bob saw it rumbling down the track, he said, "Oh, it's a London one!"

"What do you mean?" David asked. "It doesn't look like a London tram."

"Well, that's what we call the big cars. The little ones are puddle jumpers. They're more fun because they bounce all over the place."

They found seats inside the warm, steamy car and the streetcar lurched along Twelfth Street. The wheels squealed as it rounded the curve and began to cross the river on Broadway Bridge. David looked out of the window through a small patch cleared in the frost on the glass.

"I like London trams," he said. "I used to go for a ride every time we went up to London. You can go on the upper deck and get a super view. One tram goes along the Embankment and you can watch the river. It's a really big river with tugboats and barges and ships from all over the world. When the tram goes over the river there, you can look out of one side and see St. Paul's and out the other side you can see the Houses of Parliament. That's the best tram ride of all."

"You miss London, don't you David?" Mrs. Williams said.

"Yes, I do. I like London."

"Well, maybe we'll win the war soon and you can go home," Bob said.

"You'd like that, wouldn't you? You can't wait to get rid of me."

"I just meant you'd have a chance to go home."

"You must think I'm stupid."

For the rest of the trip, they sat side by side in silence. Bob felt sick. Every time it seemed as if they could be even a bit friendly, David did or said something like that. It seemed impossible for them to be friends and Bob tried to imagine what it would be like snapping and snarling at each other for years. He was glad when the streetcar stopped near the skate shop and he followed his mother into the store.

The skate shop was small and crowded. Used

skates hung from hooks all around the walls and the spaces in between were covered with old yellowing hockey calendars. A new calendar showing the Saskatoon Quakers 1940-41 team had been pinned to the wall behind the counter. The store owner came out of the back room, still carrying the skate he had been sharpening. He put it on top of the counter.

"Afternoon, Mrs. What'd you need today?"

"Skates for both of them."

"Were you looking for something new?"

"Yes," said David.

"No, used ones will be fine," Mrs. Williams said. David was fitted with a pair first and he stood in the store wobbling on bent ankles while Bob was being fitted.

"Not a skater?" the man asked David.

"I soon will be."

"That's the spirit. The Quakers could sure use you."

On the way back to the streetcar, they stopped at a drug store. Mrs. Williams bought a rubber bedsheet. David scowled when he saw it and all the way home he sat glowering out of the frosted window.

As soon as they had finished lunch, David said, "I'm going to the rink."

A lot of boys were skating on the rink in the schoolyard. Danny skated over when he saw them.

"Hey, you got skates — great!"

Bob's feet got cold as he changed into his skates and he hurried to lace them up, wiggling his toes to warm them. Danny knelt to help David with his skates. When David stepped onto the ice, his feet slipped and he fell backwards onto the pile of snow banked up around the ice.

"Nice try, Hockeybat!" one of the boys yelled. A couple of them came over to watch as David struggled up.

"Just get your balance first," Bob instructed.

"I'm trying."

"Then you can try moving. Keep your knees bent a bit. Here, I'll give you a hand."

"I'll ask when I need it, thanks."

"Suit yourself."

Bob skated off across the rink, gliding easily and quickly over the ice. He felt great, moving smoothly, cutting and turning sharply, listening to the rasp of the sharp blades and watching the shower of ice as he stopped. David was tottering around the edge of the rink with Danny skating slowly alongside talking to him. Bob began a game of "three and you're in" with some of the boys.

"Hockeybat's going great," one of them said after a while.

"I don't know about him, but I'm going home. It's too cold for me. I think my feet have broken off at the ankles," someone else said.

As it got dark and colder, the boys began to drift away from the rink. Danny skated over to Bob. He was shivering and his face had a couple of white patches on the cheeks.

"I've got to go home, I'm dying. Can you get

David off the ice? He wants to keep going but he'll kill himself."

"Let him if he wants to."

"Oh, come on, Bob. We can't just leave him here. He could get frostbite. It's getting really cold now."

They argued with David for a couple of minutes. He was shivering and his legs were shaking with tiredness, but he refused to stop and skated away from them after they had changed out of their skates.

"You'd better tell your dad."

"Yeah, he might listen to him. I hope he's home."

Bob ran all the way home. His feet stung and he was glad to reach the warmth of the kitchen. The house was full of the smell of his father's pipe.

"Dad, dad" he yelled.

"What's the racket all about?"

"It's David. He's at the rink and he won't come home. It's freezing out there. You'd better go and get him, he wouldn't listen to me or Danny."

Mr. Williams knocked out his pipe and struggled into his boots and overcoat. It was bitter cold outside and he suddenly felt angry at having to leave the house to go and fetch a boy who did not know when to come in. As he turned the corner near Albert school, he could see David skating slowly, stumbling and falling often. The boy's coat was covered in ice and snow and his scarf was thick with frost. He was alone on the ice under the glow of the streetlights.

"Good grief!" Mr. Williams began to run. "David, get over here right now," he yelled.

110

David skated toward him. The boy's legs were shaking and his whole body was shivering.

"Come home this minute! You'll kill yourself."

David did not argue and bent down to undo his laces.

"Forget that — hop on."

"No, I'm all right."

"It's too cold to argue. On my back, quick."

Mr. Williams bent down and picked up David's boots while the boy climbed onto his back. Mr. Williams began to walk as quickly as he could. He could feel David shivering on his back and the skates banged against his legs making him stumble from time to time. David's head fell onto Mr. Williams' shoulder and then his whole body sagged. David weighed no more than Bob had a couple of years ago, but the weight made Mr. Williams gasp. He carried David straight into the kitchen.

Mrs. Williams wasted no time. She took her kitchen scissors and cut the laces, then carefully pulled off David's skates and socks. His feet were white.

"Should I get some snow?" Bob asked. "You know, to rub his feet?"

"That's Jack London stuff. No, get a basin of warm water — not hot, mind," Mr. Williams said.

"I'm all right," David said, trying to stand up. His legs were trembling and he had to sit down again while Mrs. Williams took off his coat and scarf. Aunt Peg came in with a couple of blankets and wrapped them around David. Bob brought the bowl of water and Mrs. Williams tested it with her hand before David put his feet into it.

"Ow — it's too hot."

"It's just warm. It feels hot because your feet are so cold. Make him some tea, Ted. He can have that with plenty of sugar. That should help."

"Didn't anyone tell you about frostbite, David?"

"We read about Captain Scott at school."

"Remember what happened to him," Mr. Williams said.

"He didn't give up."

Mr. Williams looked at David, bundled in his blankets with his feet in the bowl of water and he laughed.

"You're a tough little customer aren't you. But you're young enough to take a couple of days to learn to skate. You don't have to do it in one day, you know."

"I just don't like being the only one who can't do it."

"Well, come and listen to the hockey broadcast," Mr. Williams said. "This year the Leafs are going to win the Stanley Cup."

"What's that?" David asked.

"Boy, you've got a lot to learn," Bob said.

They sat David in the big chair near the radiator and settled down to listen to the game. Within minutes, David had fallen asleep and Mr. Williams carried him, still wrapped in his blankets, up to bed.

David was snoring when Bob climbed into bed. The bed smelled rubbery and the sheet soon made Bob feel hot and sweaty.

"It's like sleeping in a tire. I can't wait for January," Bob thought. "Except that means Aunt Peg will be gone. I'll miss her." When Bob woke in the morning, he could smell the hot rubber sheet. They had gone the whole night without having to get up to change the bed. Bob began to laugh.

"Gee, David, you sure like to keep us guessing."

But they needed the rubber sheet the next night.

CHAPTER 13

"ANY letters for me?" David asked when he came into the house.

"No, dear, I'm sorry," Aunt Peg said.

"When will they come? I've been waiting ages."

"Perhaps there's been a holdup. I'll get Mary to ask at the committee, but you'll hear soon, I'm sure."

David grunted and went upstairs. He lay on the bed and read his old letters again. He knew them almost by heart, but he liked the British stamps and he felt better just looking at his parents' handwriting. "I hope they're all right," David thought, remembering the screaming bombs and glowing fires of the last air raid before he had left home. "I wonder what mum's doing right now." One of her letters said that she was going to train as an ambulance driver. "With you and your dad both away, I want to do my bit and so I hope they'll take me." Perhaps she was doing that. "And dad could be anywhere in North Africa," David thought, staring at the map pinned on the wall. "I wish I knew what they were doing. Why don't they write?"

"How are you, David? You look a bit downcast," Mr. Williams said when David came down to supper.

"Oh, I'm all right, Mr. Williams, thank you."

"I tell you what," Mr. Williams said to everyone, "why don't we all have our supper quickly and get down to the Tivoli before six — we could all see Charlie Chaplin."

The Great Dictator," Bob said. "Oh, that'd be swell, dad. Everyone says it's really funny. He looks just like Hitler and it's a real riot."

"It's a bit expensive, Ted," Mrs. Williams said.

"Only in the evenings. If we get there before six it's only 75¢ each. Get the jar."

Mrs. Williams went to the cupboard by the window and opened it. Bob saw David stiffen, then look down at his plate as Mrs. Williams reached up and took down the stone marmalade jar. She reached into it, and looked puzzled.

"That's odd," she said, tipping the jar to get a better look. "I'm sure there was more than this in here." Mrs. Williams spilled the money onto the counter. The coins slid over the surface, glinting in the light. "There were a couple of dollar bills in here — I know it. Where can they be?"

"Are they on the shelf?" Mr. Williams asked.

Mrs. Williams checked the shelf. "No!"

Bob stared over at David, trying to force him to look up from his plate.

"Would you like a cola, David?" Bob whispered.

"Shut up!" he hissed.

"How about some candy?"

"Tattletale, are you going to snitch?"

"What are you boys whispering about?" Mrs. Williams said. "Do either of you know anything about this?"

There was a long silence as the boys avoided each other's eye. Mr. Williams looked at them and said crossly, "If either of you do know about it, I want to hear. Mother says there's two dollars missing." When neither of them spoke, he said, "Bob, don't make me angry, now. Do you know anything about the money?"

"No, dad, I don't," Bob muttered.

"Well, David," Mr. Williams said after a pause, "perhaps you can explain."

David looked up from the table at the adults staring at him. Aunt Peg looked concerned and Mrs. Williams was still standing by the open cupboard with the empty jar in her hand.

"David, you do know something about it," Mrs. Williams said, "I can see it in your face. Why don't you tell us?"

"Of course I took it," David said angrily, pushing back his chair and jumping up. He backed away from the table until he was standing with his back to the refrigerator, glowering at everyone. "Why shouldn't I take it?"

"Because it's not yours," Mr. Williams said.

"Who says — what about the money my mum sends you?"

"What money?" Mrs. Williams said. "No one gives us money."

116

"That's not true. My mum gives the government six shillings a week but you just keep it and give me 25¢," David shouted.

"Now, just hold on, young fella," Mr. Williams said, standing up. "You watch how you speak to Mrs. Williams."

"All right, Ted," Mrs. Williams said, coming to the table and putting her hand on Mr. Williams arm. She put the empty jar on the table.

"Is that the evidence?" David shouted. "Are you going to call a bobby?" He darted away from the refrigerator and ran into the back porch.

"Come back," Mr. Williams shouted as David grabbed his coat from the hook, but Mrs. Williams kept her hand on her husband's arm as David ran from the house, banging the door behind him.

"The young imp!" Mr. Williams said. "A barefaced lie, just like that. 'I took it' and then all that nonsense about it being his. Well, he's in for it when he comes back."

"Let's hope he does," Aunt Peg said.

Mrs. Williams sat down slowly, pushing her hair back from her forehead with a tired gesture.

"No, Ted, it's not his fault really. Lots of children think we're being paid for their keep. We should have explained it better."

"We'd really get rich on $1.20 a week!" Mr. Williams grunted. "But whatever he thinks he was doing, I think he was stealing and we're going to sort that out if he's going to be living here."

"Yes, we'll have to straighten him out," Mrs.

Williams said, "but it may take a while."

David was gone a long time and Bob was sent up to bed before he came home. The three adults waited anxiously for David to return. Mr. Williams was on the verge of going to look for him when they heard David's footsteps on the path and then the back door opened.

"Good job it's not locked," Mr. Williams muttered as David stood in the kitchen doorway with his hands over his ears and his coat collar white with frost.

"Court in session? What's the verdict?" David said.

"Come in and get warm," Aunt Peg said. "I'll get you some tea."

David hung up his coat and sat down, shivering, at the table. His hands shook as he took the cup of tea.

"What are we going to do with you, David?" Mr. Williams asked.

"I don't care. You can telephone CORB and they'll take me somewhere else."

"We're not going to do that," Mrs. Williams said. "But you have to understand that we don't get anything from your mother, or anyone else, for your keep."

"So it wasn't your money you took, David," Mr. Williams said.

David looked around slowly, then dropped his eyes to the table and whispered, "I suppose I was stealing."

"I think so," Mr. Williams said.

"But you aren't going to send me away?"

"No."

"What about the money?"

"How much did you take?"

"I don't know. There were a couple of dollar bills, and I took some five cent and ten cent coins."

"Shall we say $2.50?" Mr. Williams asked.

David nodded.

"Well, you'll have to pay it back — out of your allowance — and we can find you some extra jobs to do until you're all square. Then we'll forget it. Okay?"

"Okay, Mr. Williams."

"Get up to bed now, David; fresh start in the morning."

The three adults watched David climb the stairs. Then Peg poured them all more tea.

"He's such a long way from home," Peg said.

"Well, he's got a new home here, let's hope he realizes it," Mr. Williams said. "And I hope he doesn't do anything like that again."

"But it's hard, isn't it, fitting into someone else's home?"

"Is that how you feel, Peg?" Mrs. Williams said, looking at her sister with surprise.

"Now, Mary, you're very good to me and I'm very happy here. But I am looking forward to being in my own place with Arthur again."

David opened the bedroom door.

"Oh, you decided to come back, did you?"

119

"Yes, I knew you couldn't get on without me. You'd have no one to tell tales on, would you?"

"What'll you do now? No more playing Mr. Big Shot after school with the colas, eh? We missed Charlie Chaplin. Thanks."

"Sorry, Bobbie, your dad says you won't be getting rid of me soon, even if you do snitch on me."

"Who'd take you, anyway?"

CHAPTER 14

DAVID did not drop in at Mr. Timmins' store anymore. Every recess he skated round and round the rink, not playing shinny but concentrating on learning how to be a good skater. He stayed on after school, skating until suppertime if it wasn't too cold. The other boys would often give him tips or shout encouragement, and "Hockeybat" made progress every day. Every day, too, David would come home and ask, "Any letters?", then grab the paper and read about the war. He anxiously looked for news about the air raids on Britain and the campaign planned in Africa for sometime in December.

A few days after the discovery of the stolen money, Aunt Peg came into the kitchen after supper with a big pile of paper strips and a couple of pots of paste.

"Okay, boys, time to make the Christmas decorations," she said, putting everything down on the table. "Have you made paper chains, David?"

" 'Course I have. We have them at home every year."

"Good, then let's get cracking."

They sat around the table, carefully pasting the end of each strip and threading it through a loop of the chain before sticking the ends together. Peg's loops were neat and regular. At first the boys' loops were crooked and paste oozed out when they squeezed the paper together. They improved as they went along and the chains began to grow over the table and down onto the floor. Mrs. Williams played Christmas carols on the piano.

"Hard to believe it'll soon be Christmas," Aunt Peg said. "It'll be the second one of the war."

"And my first away from home," David said. "I wonder how many more there'll be?"

"A sight fewer if the Americans would get into the war," Aunt Peg said.

"Why don't they, Auntie?" Bob said. "We got in as soon as it started, why don't they?"

"Oh, they never do," David sneered. "My dad says it was the same in the last war. They waited until it was nearly over before they got in. Then they go around saying they won the war."

"Well, they're not the same as us, are they?" Aunt Peg said. "Most of us care about what goes on in Britain. They don't."

"Well, they jolly well ought to," David said. "Hitler will get them next if he finishes us off, won't he?"

"Yes, I expect that's why Mr. Roosevelt is sending so many guns and things to England."

"I bet he's doing it to make money. That's what they did last time," David said.

"Anyway, we're not going to lose, are we," Bob said and they all nodded and smiled.

"Time to pop the corn." Aunt Peg went to the stove and put some butter in the pan.

"Pop the corn?" David said.

"Haven't you ever done that? It's fun," said Bob.

The boys stood at the stove and watched the butter melt, then Peg poured in the corn and put on the lid.

"That's not very much. Is there enough for all of us?" David said.

"Just shake the pan," Peg said, "gently."

David took hold of the pan and began to shake it. When the first grain popped and pinged against the lid, David's eyebrows shot up in surprise. Soon the grains were popping against the lid like a machine gun and David grinned and shook the pan more quickly.

"Should be finished," Peg said, and as David snatched off the lid, a grain of corn popped and shot up into the air, landing on the floor. David laughed.

"Golly, the whole pan's full. What do we do with it now?"

"We're going to put it on thread and we'll use it to decorate the tree," Aunt Peg said.

"Most of it." Bob winked at David.

They were sitting at the table eating popcorn and threading it when the front doorbell rang. Mrs. Williams left the piano.

"Mrs. Smith, do come in."

"What does she want?" David asked with a scowl.

"David, can you come here, please?" Mrs. Williams called from the front room.

"This is going to be a really nice Christmas," David muttered. He stood up, pulling the popcorn thread off the table, and stamped out of the kitchen.

"You remember Mrs. Smith, don't you, David?"

"Why is she here? You sent for her, didn't you? You said you weren't going to send me away. I think you're rotten."

"Whatever's the matter, David?" Mrs. Smith asked. "Why are you so worked up?"

"We didn't send for Mrs. Smith, David. She came here to give you something."

"Is there anything wrong, David? Would you like to talk to me privately? You can if there's any sort of problem, you know," Mrs. Smith said.

There was quiet in the front room. Bob and Peg looked at one another over the kitchen table and Aunt Peg raised her eyebrows.

"No, thank you, Mrs. Smith. Everything's all right, thank you."

"Now that's good to hear. But remember you can always phone me if you want a talk. No one ever needs to know. Mrs. Williams understands that. Anyway, I've come here with good news for you."

Mrs. Smith reached into her bag and pulled out a parcel and a packet of letters.

"I really must apologize, David. These letters have been going to Plunkett, to your old address. They just let them pile up there and only sent them on when we phoned. It won't happen again, dear."

"Oh, super!"

David snatched the parcel and packet and ran upstairs without another word. They heard the bedroom door slam and Peg and Bob smiled at each other. Mrs. Williams brought Mrs. Smith into the kitchen for tea and cookies.

"It's always such a pleasure to see the children happy," Mrs. Smith said as she left. "You must find it very rewarding, Mary."

"It does have its moments, Pearl."

After Mrs. Smith had gone, Mr. Williams came home, looking cold and tired.

"This weather!" he complained as Mrs. Williams brought him his supper from the oven. "I don't think I'll be home for supper 'til after Christmas. Every schedule's wrecked." He looked around the kitchen. "Where's David? I hope he's not out skating. I don't think I could carry him home tonight."

"He's upstairs, dad. He got some letters from home."

"Well, thank goodness for that, he's waited long enough."

David came downstairs, grinning from ear to ear.

"Looks like you had good news, David," Mr. Williams laughed.

"Oh, it's super, Mr. Williams. I had letters from mum and dad and everything's fine. Mum says they had a bomb in the next street that blew all the windows out of our house, but she's all right. They had to put brown paper up for days until the windows were mended."

"And your father?"

"He's in Cairo. He says he was ill for a while, but it worked out well because when he got better they made him a driver and now he's been chosen to be General Wavell's own driver."

"Wavell! The Commander-in-Chief! Is that true?" Bob said without thinking.

"Of course it's true," David said. "I'll show you the letter. Dad used to be a chauffeur for Lady Morton."

"Wavell — that'll be interesting work," Mr. Williams said.

"Dad says things are really busy, the big push is on. He says it's a lot better than banging around in a tank. Most of the time he drives a big Humber staff car."

"I'm so glad for you, David," Mr. Williams said, "good news for Christmas."

They all went into the front room and sang carols until bedtime. David had a very good voice and sang the carols well, even doing the descant on some of them.

"You've been in a choir, haven't you, David?" Mrs. Williams said.

"I've given myself away," David grinned.

"Wait until I tell Mrs. McIntosh. You'll be in the choir before you know it," Bob teased. "Don't see why I should go to choir practice by myself all the time."

They sang happily and afterwards the two boys talked for a long time in bed. Bob was half asleep when he heard a strange sound from David's side of the bed.

Bob listened, puzzled. "David, is something wrong?"

There was a muffled noise from David.

"David, you're crying, aren't you. What's wrong?"

David rolled over onto his back and began to cry louder, sniffing and rubbing his face with the bed clothes. Bob lifted himself onto his elbow. He could see the tears smeared over David's face, shining in the dim light.

"What's wrong, David? Should I get mum?"

"No, don't. I'm all right, really."

"Why are you crying, then?"

"I just miss everyone. I miss mum and dad, and I miss Toby, my dog, and my gran and grandpa and oh, everybody. All my friends."

Bob lay down and stared up at the ceiling. A lot of memories came back to him, suddenly.

"I know what you mean, David. I felt like that when I went to camp the first time."

"Camp," David sobbed. "That's just a couple of weeks. I'm going to be here for years."

"You've got friends here, David, you'll be okay."

"Friends. No one will be my friend now that I can't buy colas and sweets."

"Danny's your friend. He always says you're okay."

"I like Danny. He knows how I feel."

"So do I, David. I mean I just told you I did."

"Stop pretending, Bob. I know you hate me."

"I don't," Bob said indignantly. "I was looking forward to having a brother."

"You laughed at me when I got here."

"Laughed at you?"

"I saw you. When Mrs. Smith brought me here. You laughed at me and you've been beastly ever since. And you said those things about my father getting killed."

"I wasn't laughing at you, David. And I'm sorry about what I said. It just slipped out. I didn't mean it, honest I didn't. I felt terrible as soon as I said it. I talked to Auntie Peg about it and everything. I'm sorry."

Gradually David stopped crying and lay quietly before rolling over onto his side. The boys began to drift off to sleep and Bob was almost asleep when David said, "Bob?"

"Yeah?"

"Bob, if you tell anyone about me crying and everything, I'll kill you, I really will."

"I won't tell anyone, David. Honest."

"Well, just remember, I'll kill you. I mean it."

"Sure, David. Good night."

CHAPTER 15

BOB was eating breakfast when David came downstairs in the morning. The two boys looked at each other shyly, almost as if they were meeting for the first time. Mrs. Williams brought David his porridge.

"I don't think I want any, thank you, Mrs. Williams."

"You need something on a cold morning, David."

"I don't feel very well."

Mrs. Williams put her hand on David's forehead. "Back to bed, David. You've got a fever. I'll phone Dr. Lawrence. You get off to school, Bob."

David had the measles. He was annoyed at the news. "That's what little kids get," he said. "I'm too old for measles."

"Well, as you didn't get it when you were small, you get a holiday now. There's quite an epidemic in Saskatoon at the moment," Dr. Lawrence said to Mrs. Williams. "Hope it doesn't spoil too many Christmas concerts. Bob's had them, so he'll be fine.

You'll soon be well again, David — if you stay in bed — but don't do anything foolish, young man. Measles can be tricky sometimes."

For a couple of days David was very ill. His temperature stayed high and he was covered with a red rash. His eyes hurt and Mrs. Williams kept the curtains drawn in the bedroom. Bob slept downstairs on the sofa during the worst days of David's illness and he stayed home from school too. "No sense taking the chance you'll spread it around," his mother said. Bob did not complain. He spent the time downstairs in the workshop. When he finished cutting out the sewing basket, his father helped him to glue it together. "You've done a good job, Bob. You're getting to be a real woodworker," Mr. Williams said. Bob felt proud and got up enough nerve to make his father a pipe rack over the next two days that he was home.

As David got better, he became bored. He lay on the sofa listening to the radio, waiting for the BBC and CBC news broadcasts and listening to the American soap operas. David's eyes still hurt, but he was eager to hear about the war, so Bob read the news to him when he got home from his paper route. For half an hour before supper, Bob would read the articles about General Wavell's campaign in North Africa, and the boys would talk about defeating the Italians. Each night, Bob moved the pins in the map of North Africa to show the position of the two armies. For the first time since David had arrived, the boys began to feel like friends.

Bob went back to school before David. Everyone was busy rehearsing for the Christmas concert, practising their choral pieces and skits. Bob was bored with the rehearsals. He was scheduled to play Mendelsohn, so there wasn't much for him to do when his class was rehearsing. When Mr. Greenshields saw Bob sitting around one day, he recruited him for the stage crew. After that, Bob spent all his time sawing, hammering, and painting. He was often allowed to stay at work when the others went back to the classroom for regular lessons.

"Too valuable a man to lose," Mr. Greenshields said. "He really knows one end of a hammer from another." So, instead of dragging, the last days of the term raced by.

One evening, Danny came over to play Monopoly. The boys sat on the floor in the bedroom. David was wearing his pyjamas and dressing gown.

"You look okay to me," Danny said. "Sure you're not faking?"

"I did it all with red paint," David said, "because school was so boring."

"What are you doing for the show?"

"Oh, they've asked me to sing a couple of songs. Why is there so much fuss about the show, anyway?"

"Everyone comes. It's the big event of the year. You'll see, the auditorium is packed. Everyone's granny is there — the teachers really get nervous. Last year Mr. Martin got so wound up he drank half a bottle of whiskey to calm himself down. You should have heard the songs he was singing in the staff room. They were something. He joined the navy last January," Danny laughed.

"Shake the dice," Bob said, "you're stalling just because you're near Boardwalk."

"How many more Christmases do you think the war will last?" David asked as Danny rolled the dice and moved his marker around the corner to collect his $200.

"I don't know. Sometimes I hope it'll go on long enough so I can get into it," Danny said. "Did you see what the Nazi's did in Warsaw last week? They built a big wall around blocks and blocks of the city and now they've told all the Jews they've got to live in there. They need a pass just to get in or out.

"You never say much about your uncle anymore, Danny. What's happening with his committee?" Bob asked.

"Nothing much," Danny said. "They keep getting letters like the one you got from the Prime Minister's office. I wish I was old enough to be in the war like Fred."

"Bob says we shouldn't bomb the Nazis," David said.

"I never!"

"Yes, you did. You said it was wrong to bomb Berlin."

"I just asked about it. Dad was going on about Coventry and I couldn't see what's so different."

"*They're* different," Danny said, "the Germans." Bob looked at him and Danny looked away. A silence fell until David picked up the dice and rolled them.

"Well, I jolly well hope it's over soon, even if I don't get into it. I want everything back to normal."

"Why? Don't you like it here?" Bob asked with a grin. David pushed Bob off balance. Bob threatened to push David, too.

"You wouldn't hit a sick man, would you?" David whined.

"Okay, save your strength to push that marker around. I want you on Boardwalk."

"It should be Mayfair," David said as he counted off the spaces. "Oh, what rotten luck, Bobbie, I seem to have landed on Go."

"Bobbie? You want to know what it's like to be really sick, little Davy?" Bob grinned.

David won the game, which made him very happy. Later, Bob went downstairs to see Danny out.

"You guys didn't fight once," Danny said as he tied his scarf. "I kept waiting for it; what's happened?"

"Oh, Hockeybat's okay when you get to know him."

Bob watched as his friend bundled himself into his coat and pulled on the flying helmet.

"You really look like a pilot in that helmet," Bob said.

"I just wish I was older. Then I could be one instead of just reading about it. I wish I could do something."

"I know, especially when you read a story like that one from Warsaw."

"It's really scary, Bob. Imagine living inside a wall; it would be like jail. Grandpa says something terrible is going to happen."

"Maybe the war will end soon. Things look good in Africa."

"It's a long way from Africa to Berlin."

Bob let Danny out and went back upstairs. David was sitting at the desk writing a letter home and Bob began to pick up the Monopoly money and cards.

"Danny's really worried about the news from Warsaw. He was talking about it before he left. He says his grandfather thinks something terrible will happen."

"I bet he's right. I had two Jewish boys from Austria in my class. Their parents sent them to Britain when Hitler invaded Austria because they were scared of what he was going to do."

"What happened to them?"

"Well, they heard from their parents a couple of times and then they never heard from them again."

"What will they do? Did they come to Canada with you?"

"No."

"Why not?"

"I don't know. Hans said they couldn't come to Canada until their parents signed the forms."

"But..." Bob could not think of anything to say to that. He finished tidying up the game and put it away. David finished his letters to home.

CHAPTER 16

DAVID went back to school a couple of days later. His friends were glad to see him and he was soon back on the rink. He was a little shaky after being off the ice for so long, but quickly improved.

"Hockeybat's pretty good on the skates," Bill Kindrachuk said to Bob. "I bet he could play in the league next year if he wanted."

"He's a bit small, Bill."

"Maybe, but he's already got some moves. We can show him some stuff during the holidays. He learns quickly."

"He's learned to keep out of Greg's way," Bob laughed as they watched David check and turn away from Greg. David skated over to them and stopped, but lost his balance and fell into the snow bank, his arms plunged into the snow up to the elbows.

"Real smooth, Hockeybat," Bill said, hauling David up. "Like I was saying to Bob, we'll have to show you a few moves. We'll make a hockey player out of you yet!"

"I'm doing all right," David snapped.

"No one said you weren't," Bill grinned, "you just need fine tuning!"

"And you don't have to grin like that, Bobbie," David said, skating off across the rink brushing snow from his sleeves.

"A tad touchy, ain't he."

"Sometimes."

David caught up to Bob on the way home from school and walked along with him.

"Aren't you skating?" Bob asked.

"I'm tired. Anyway, I thought I could give you a hand with the papers, if you still want. I need the money, if you're willing to split it."

"Sure, we can split it. But not the Christmas tips," Bob added quickly. "I've worked a year for those."

"Okay. We'll split them next Christmas, though."

"Boy, that's planning ahead."

"Well, you have to sometimes."

The news in the paper was good. They read snatches of the story on the front page as they hurried from house to house. At home, they quickly opened the paper on the kitchen table and sat side by side while they read the whole story.

"What's it all about, boys?" Aunt Peg asked. "Must be something special."

"It is. The British have just won a big victory against the Italians. It says they've captured Sidi-Barrani."

"Where?"

"Funny sort of name. Do you think it's Siddeye, Sydee, Sidi?"

"Bahrany, Bahrahny, Barrannee," David said.

They read Aunt Peg the story. The British army had surprised the Italians and whole armies were surrendering to General Wavell. Sidi-Barrani had been captured and more victories were expected shortly. Egypt was safer from the enemy than it had been at any time since the war began in the desert.

"Why, that is wonderful news," Aunt Peg said. "Perhaps this war will be over sooner than we thought."

"And my dad must be driving Wavell all over the place. I bet it's exciting. Of course, if the Germans get into the war there, it'll be different. Dad always said they were more worried about the Germans than about the Italians, especially after the Germans pushed us out of France in the summer."

"Well, I think we should be glad for the good news, and not worry about what might be. It's the best way," Aunt Peg said, "and in time for Christmas, too."

At supper time it felt even more like Christmas. For once, Mr. Williams got home early and when he came into the house, he was carrying a Christmas tree.

"Give me a hand," he called as waves of cold air rolled in. "Get it inside while I get the door. Sure glad it wasn't locked," he said smiling at David who blushed.

"I haven't done that for ages, Mr. Williams," David said as he helped Bob carry the tree into the front room. They rested it against the wall while Mrs. Williams found the stand and they all helped put it up. They left the tree to thaw while they ate supper and talked happily about the news from Africa.

"And the great thing is, David's dad's as safe as he can be," Mr. Williams said. "Not too many field marshals get killed in a war. We found that out last time."

After supper Mr. Williams brought up the step ladder and they hung the paper chains across the ceiling and around the walls. Then they put the popcorn strings and the decorations on the Christmas tree.

"Here you are, David. I'll hold the ladder. You can put the star on top," Mr. Williams said.

"But I..."Bob said, then stopped. He had put the star there every year since he was very small and Mr. Williams had had to hold him up in the air to do it. Now Bob stood with his mother and Aunt Peg as David carefully climbed up the step ladder and leaned over to fix the star in place. Everyone clapped when he succeeded and Mrs. Williams sat down at the piano to play Christmas music.

"Why don't we have any of those Japanese oranges, mum?" Bob asked. "We always have them at Christmas."

"I can't get them, Bob. They told me the people in B.C. are boycotting Japan. They won't import the oranges this year."

"Why are they doing that, mum?"

"They're upset about the treaty Japan signed with Germany."

"Does that mean the Japanese will join the war?" David asked. "Gosh, I hope they don't."

"Oh, let's not even think about it — let's just sing," Mrs. Williams suggested. Then they all sang carols and ate the first of the Christmas baking.

"You cut Christmas cake in very small pieces here," David said. "At home, before the war, we used to have great big slices of it. With marzipan and hard icing on top."

"Oh, I think Bob gets through the same amount, bit by bit, whatever way you slice it," Mr. Williams laughed.

"You're not so slow yourself, Ted," Mrs. Williams said. "Now who can that be?" she asked as the front doorbell rang.

"One way to find out," Mr. Williams said. "Answer it, Bob."

There was a stranger at the door when Bob opened it. "Telegram," he said. "Sign here," and he pushed a notebook and pencil at Bob. The man gave Bob a small envelope, then turned and walked down the path. Bob watched him go and suddenly felt weak at the knees. He could hear the piano and David singing. Bob did not want to go back into the room.

"Who is it, Bob?" Mr. Williams called out. "Come in and shut the door. We're freezing in here."

Bob walked slowly back into the bright front room. His mother stopped playing the piano and turned to look at him. Suddenly, it seemed that everyone was staring at the envelope in Bob's hand.

"A telegram! Who is it for, Bob?" Aunt Peg said, trying not to let her voice shake.

Bob looked at the envelope. The name scrawled there was D. Harris.

"So it's not Uncle Arthur," he thought. Immediately he felt guilty at the relief which flooded through him. Aloud he said, "It's for David," and he walked across the room and handed him the telegram.

David sat down and stared at the envelope, as if he were checking the name. He stared at it for a long time.

"Would you like me to open it for you, dear? You'll have to know what it says sometime."

"No thanks, Peg. I'll do it."

David took a knife from the table and carefully slit the envelope. Then he reached into it and took out the paper. He unfolded the paper as carefully as he had opened the envelope and pressed it flat with his hand. Bob could see the dark blue design at the top of the sheet and the large purple letters of the message as David slowly read them.

David began to smile and everyone looked at him in surprise.

"Listen," he said. " 'David Harris. Mother will broadcast CBC six p.m. twenty-third December. Repeat broadcast two p.m. twenty-sixth. Merry Christmas. Jopson. CORB.' I'm going to hear mum on the wireless! Isn't that wizard news?"

"Oh, David. Straight from home. That's

wonderful." Mrs. Williams gave him a hug as David excitedly stood up. He let her hug him without protesting, then began dancing around the room when she let him go.

"Marvellous, the things they can do these days," Mr. Williams said. "I heard they've fixed it up so some of the guest children can talk to their parents. Maybe we'll manage that here soon."

"Oh, that'd be fantastic. I could tell her everything — about skating, and the boys at school, and hockey, and oh, about how jolly silly I've been acting."

Mrs. Williams smiled at him and took his hand.

"Least said, soonest mended. Let's have a few more carols."

The boys were still excited when they went up to bed. They changed into their pyjamas and chatted happily about the news from Africa. They even managed to find Sidi Barrani on the map.

"It looks like a port," Bob said.

"Gosh. Maybe dad's gone for a swim. I wish I could do that — I like the beach."

"I bet we could get to the lake in the summer. There are beaches there."

"Oh, you have to see the sea, Bob; there's nothing like it. It's super. We used to go all the time."

"It's going to be swell, hearing from your mother."

They talked for a while in bed before they calmed down. Just before he drifted off to sleep, Bob thought he heard a noise from David and he whispered, "You okay, David?"

"Yes, thanks."

"I just thought I heard something."

There was a pause for a moment and then David said fiercely, "Look, I'm not going to blubber, you know."

"Huh?"

"Afraid I'll cry again? If he blubbered over the letters, what do you think he'd do about a telegram? Is that what you're thinking?"

"No, David."

"Well, I put on a good show for you once. You can't expect it all the time."

"Jeez, David, sorry I spoke."

Now wide awake, Bob lay for a long time staring at the ceiling. "What was that all about?" he asked himself, but he could not find an answer. David lay awake, too, feeling foolish and angry with himself for blowing up. "I dunno why I did, really," he thought. Then, as he began to fall asleep, he whispered, "Good night, Bob. Sorry."

"Good night, David."

They changed the sheet quietly about two o'clock in the morning, without waking Mrs. Williams.

CHAPTER 17

THE twenty-third was the last day of school and the day of the concert. Things at school were chaotic, as classes rehearsed their pieces for the evening. Bob spent most of the day in the auditorium, helping Mr. Greenshields with the scenery. The classroom teachers were fussing, some of them frantic, but Mr. Greenshields kept saying, "It'll be all right on the night."

Bob did manage to get to the class party, but he missed the grade seven rehearsals and did not see David until after school.

"Come on, Bob. Let's get the papers done. We've got to be home before six. We can't miss the broadcast," David said, hurrying along Clarence.

"I can do them, David, you just go home if you like."

"Oh, no. I'd like you to hear it, too."

They were home in plenty of time to eat supper early. They wanted to go straight to the school after the broadcast. David could not eat, but pushed his meat loaf around on the plate.

"I'm sorry, Mrs. Williams. I'm just too excited. I'll eat it later, honest."

"Why don't you just go and listen to the radio, David, and we'll clear up in here."

David jumped up and ran into the front room. A program of dance music came on the radio. Mrs. Williams began to hum.

"Pity your dad won't be here. He said he'll try to be at the school later."

Bob's excitement matched David's. When Bob joined David in the front room, David was sitting at the radio with his ear almost against the speaker. Bob sprawled on the floor in his usual place.

"Why don't they get on with it?" David said. "They've been playing this music for hours."

Aunt Peg and Mrs. Williams came into the room and settled down in their chairs. They both began to knit.

"It's a pity you boys don't knit," Mrs. Williams said. "It's a wonderful way to relax."

"Come on, come on," David muttered to the radio.

The music faded at last and the announcer came on.

"Good evening ladies and gentlemen, boys and girls. The CBC is very pleased to be able to bring you a special show this holiday season. Christmas is a time for families, but as you know, the war has divided many families. Some of those separated from their families are our guest children, safe among us and away from the bombing and the war, but sadly separated from their mothers and fathers."

"Isn't he ever going to stop?" David said impatiently.

"We know how much these boys and girls must be missing their families and friends, and we are happy that the miracle of radio allows us to bring greetings to just a few of the children now living among us for the duration."

"Oh, get on with it," David groaned.

"Tonight we go on a voyage across Canada, for every province is home to some guest children. Our Canadian hospitality stretches from sea to sea through all nine provinces. Join us now in Halifax and listen as we bring greetings to two children in Nova Scotia from their parents in Old Scotland."

"At last!" David said, huddling closer to the radio.

The greetings worked their way across the country, through the Maritimes and central Canada, on to Winnipeg, and at last the announcer said, "And now to Saskatoon, where David Harris is a welcome guest. David is the son of Mrs. Ada Harris. His father is serving with the British Army somewhere in Africa."

"Hello, David."

"It's mum!"

"We were so glad to get your letter and to hear that you're settling down nicely now. We know you'll be happy in your new home. Dad's all right now, he's out of the hospital and sends you his love. We all miss you so much this Christmas, dear, and we're glad you're safe from the bombing. Please thank the Williamses for looking after you. Granny and grampa send you their love, too, and Merry Christmas. Write soon. Goodbye for now, love."

"Mr. and Mrs. John..." the announcer was saying as Mrs. Williams turned off the radio. David lay flat on his back staring up at the ceiling with a half smile on his face. Suddenly everyone was smiling. No one said anything, but just let David enjoy whatever thoughts he was having. It was a few moments before he sat up.

"Wasn't that super? She was using her posh voice, but it really sounded just like her. I've never heard anyone I know on the wireless before."

"And it was so clear. She might have been in the room with us," Aunt Peg said.

"I wish she was," David said, then he blushed and said, "I mean, you're all kind..."

"Come on, boys," Mrs. Williams said, "time to be going."

David seemed glad of the chance to jump up and get ready for the walk to school. They were soon hurrying toward Albert School. People were coming from all directions, bundled into coats and scarfs against the cold wind. A crowd was waiting to climb the steps to the main entrance.

"Crikey, where's everyone coming from?" David said.

"Oh, everyone comes to the school concert," Bob told him proudly. "It'll be the biggest show they've seen since Gracie Fields sang here in the summer."

"Gracie Fields?"

"You know her. She's the biggest star in the

Empire. And she sang here at the Arena. Five thousand people were there. You must have heard of her — she's English."

"Yes, I've heard my mum talk about her," David said. He seemed to be laughing under his scarf, but Bob was not sure.

They were squeezed by the crowd and pushed up the steps and then through the door. The boys went downstairs to their classrooms while Aunt Peg and Mrs. Williams made their way to the auditorium on the first floor. The school was brightly lit and dressed with Christmas decorations. The only seats left in the packed auditorium were near the back. Men were even sitting on the windowsills. People chatted cheerfully to their neighbours despite the heat in the room, and everyone was in a good mood. Younger children — brothers and sisters of the performers — squirmed on their parent's laps or wriggled away to crawl under the chairs.

"Can you see?" Mrs. Williams asked Peg.

"I'm certainly glad they'll be up on stage," Peg said.

The concert began. The curtains opened shakily, and the children from the first grade peered into the crowd, trying to spot their parents. Some of them waved.

As the evening progressed, beards fell off, lines were forgotten and there were long pauses and frantic whisperings from behind the closed curtains. The scenery flapped and swayed but never fell down.

The audience applauded every act, but by the time

the older children appeared, some people were beginning to look impatiently at their watches.

Bob spent his time helping Mr. Greenshields. In fact, Bob was one of the loudest whisperers behind the closed curtains as he and the rest of the stage crew struggled with scenery and props. Working kept his mind off his performance. When the Principal announced that Bob was going to play the piano, someone had to call him. The piano was on the floor, not the stage, so neither Mrs. Williams nor Aunt Peg could see Bob, but they could hear him. Mrs. Williams looked relieved when he finished.

"At least he didn't get lost in the middle," she said.

"Oh, Mary, you know he did very well," Peg laughed.

Bob stood in the wings watching as the grades seven and eight classes did their skit. It was full of carefully disguised references to the teachers which made the students giggle, but left the audience confused.

"To close our show for 1940," the Principal announced, "we're very lucky to have one of the guest children now staying with us in Saskatoon. David Harris is a guest child with Mr. and Mrs. Williams and he is in grade seven. He's going to sing a couple of songs many of you will have heard this summer, 'Sally' and 'The Biggest Aspidistra in the World,' two of Gracie Fields' most popular songs."

"And he let me tell him who she was!" Bob grinned. "I'll fix him."

When the curtain opened, David looked out over the audience and then said, "Eeh, but it's lovely to be

148

back in Saskatoon. You're all such champion folk."
He sounded just like Gracie Fields and the audience
laughed. Then David nodded at the pianist, as
though she was a real pianist and not just Miss Peel,
and launched into "Sally". His voice soared up and
filled the hall and people who had been shifting in
their seats or drifting out of the auditorium stopped
to listen. When David finished the song, the audience
applauded loudly. David smiled and launched into
"The Biggest Aspidistra in the World." Between
verses, he cartwheeled around the stage and he even
worked "Saskatoon" into one of the verses. The
applause got even louder after that and David
bowed. Then someone shouted, "More," and soon
people all over the hall joined in, "More, More!"

"There now, didn't I say you were champion folk?
Righto. I'll sing one more, but only if thee all join in.
I bet you all know 'The Army, the Navy and Air
Force.'"

Miss Peel didn't have the music, but David led the
whole audience in the song and then cartwheeled off
stage as the curtains closed and everyone cheered.

Danny and Bob found David with a couple of
boys from his class. David's shirt was wet with
sweat, but he looked very happy.

"You were sensational, David," Danny said. "You
didn't do all that in rehearsal."

"No. Well, I wasn't sure how they'd like it. So I
saved it."

"That was swell, David. I guess you had heard of
Gracie Fields," Bob grinned.

"Sorry about that," David laughed. "My mum

really is a fan of hers. Mum used to do a turn on the halls and she sort of taught me that act. I thought I'd surprise you."

Parents came up to congratulate David and finally the Williamses and Aunt Peg pushed through the crush to join in. The three boys wandered off, happy and relieved that school was over for a while. People began to leave and Danny's parents came to find him.

"Say goodbye, Danny," Mrs. Miller said.

"So long, guys. See you in 1941," Danny said.

"You going away?"

"Yeah, David. We usually go to Winnipeg for the holidays. See you next year, okay?"

"I'll be here," David said quietly.

It was late when they left the school. They hurried through the quiet streets and filed up the path to the back door. They could hear the planes circling the airport, the noise of their engines clear in the night air.

"Even at Christmas," Peg said, "they're still practising."

"Let's hope there won't be many more Christmases that they have to," Mrs. Williams said as they opened the door.

CHAPTER 18

DAVID slept in the next morning, but Bob had to go to choir practice. Afterward, he walked downtown. He stopped on the bridge to look at the ice covered river. Far downstream, he could see the high railway bridge where David had run away from the train. It seemed like a long time ago. Bob hurried along Fourth Avenue, turning the corner to Eaton's. The store was crowded with last minute shoppers. Tinsel was wound around the columns which rose to the ceiling and gold and silver decorations sparkled in the lights all over the big store. Bob felt happy as he hurried down the marble stairs and into the basement. He quickly found what he wanted. The clerk looked tired, but she smiled and said, "Getting your Christmas money spent early? This is one of our Christmas specials."

"It's a present for a friend. He's from England."

"One of the guest children, is he? Does he know about these?"

"I'll show him."

Bob found a big bottle of eau de cologne for Aunt Peg and then splurged by riding the streetcar home. He stayed on the car as it passed Albert School, checking to see if David was in the schoolyard. He saw him there, skating backwards slowly, but well under control. Bob jumped off the car a couple of stops later and doubled back to the house.

"Auntie Peg," Bob called as he pushed the back door open, "can I hide David's present in your room?"

"Of course you can, dear. As long as it's not alive!"

"You've never forgotten those mice, have you?"

"Well you nearly got us evicted, letting them loose in our apartment. How could I forget?"

"Yeah, and we never did find Mickey, did we?"

After supper Aunt Peg gave David a small package. "Open it," she said. David broke the string and pulled off the tissue paper, then unrolled a big red felt sock. DAVID was stitched in white letters down the front and there were bells around the top.

"Oh, I say, how super. At home, we just hung up one of our own socks. This is really nice."

"I hope Santa Claus can find you," Bob said, "I mean, you've moved around a bit, haven't you?"

"Oh, that's all right, I wrote to him."

They all went to St. James for the midnight service. The children in the choir were excited, but Mrs. McIntosh kept them under control and they all sang well. Bob always liked the Christmas Eve service. It was dark and cold outside and the little church seemed extra warm and bright. During the prayers for the men and women who were away from home, a special quiet came over the congregation. Bob thought of Uncle Arthur and Fred and, quite suddenly, of Mr. and Mrs. Harris. All four of them were in danger. It made Saskatoon seem very safe.

The boys hurried upstairs as soon as they got home. They could hear the adults talking and laughing in the kitchen.

Very early in the morning, Bob awoke when he heard his mother's alarm go off. He heard her going downstairs. The radio went on and Bob knew she was listening to the King's broadcast. When he was very small, he sometimes tried to go down and listen with her, but he had always been brought back to bed and told to go to sleep. Bob heard the quiet murmur of the stuttering British voice and drifted off to sleep. It was nearly seven o'clock when he woke again. David was awake.

"Can we go down now?"

"It should be all right."

They went downstairs and Bob turned on the light. Although they pretended not to be too eager about opening their stockings, they soon had the contents spread all over the floor. There were balloons, games, and a couple of small toys in the socks, an orange in the heel and candy in the toe. Each sock had a bright new quarter in the toe.

"Canadian money." David spun the coin in the air. "How does Father Christmas keep track of everything?"

"You think you're pretty smart, don't you," Bob laughed, giving David a push. The coin fell on the rug and the boys scrambled for it, pushing each other and rolling round on the floor. Mr. Williams came into the room.

"Come on, boys, give your mother a chance. And Merry Christmas."

The three of them got breakfast trays ready for Aunt Peg and Bob's mum.

"We always bring her breakfast in bed on Christmas Day — it's a tradition."

They took the trays up and wished everyone a happy Christmas.

"When do you open your presents?" David asked Bob after breakfast as he looked at the pile of parcels under the tree.

"Not 'til this afternoon sometime."

"That's hours!"

"I know. It's crazy, but that's how gran likes it so that's what we do."

"You boys should go for a walk, get out of the house for a bit," Mr. Williams said in a way that made it more an order than a suggestion. They were glad to go because it was a beautiful day. The trees were covered in a thick hoarfrost which sparkled in the clear sun. The sky was a pale blue against the snow and the air was fresh and crisp.

"Gosh, it really is like a Christmas card. I've never seen anything like this at home."

They went down to the University as they had on David's first Sunday in Saskatoon. They walked along the narrow path until Bob lost his footing on the ice and slid all the way down the hill at Devil's Dip. David followed him, and hauled him out of the snow.

"That snow is pretty cold," David said.

"You get used to it."

"My mum says you get used to anything," David said as he led the way over the small wooden bridge.

"Even you?"

"That's funny, Bob," David said but he did not seem to mind.

The boys walked along the river bank high above the frozen Saskatchewan River. At the railway embankment they paused, and Bob looked at David.

"Come on," David said, scrambling up the slope. "What are you waiting for?"

As they stood in the centre of the bridge looking down, David said, "It's a pretty small town, isn't it?"

"Yeah, but it's bigger than Plunkett, so you've nothing to complain about. What's so special about big cities, anyway?" Bob asked.

"Ever been to one?"

"No, I've always lived in Saskatoon."

"Well, you'll have to go to one to find out."

"Yeah. Well, I like Saskatoon. I don't care what you think."

"I won't start anything," David said solemnly, holding up his hands. "I want to be allowed to stay until spring breakup. I hear it's simply super."

"Don't push your luck, David. It won't be Christmas every day," Bob laughed.

They hurried home along the other side of the river and up the University bridge, eager to be out of the cold. The house was full of people when they arrived. Bob introduced David to family friends and relatives. Everyone wanted to know what he thought of Canada and what the war had been like in Britain.

"I'm glad we can have David here, away from the bombing," Mrs. Williams said as she brought the boys over to Bob's grandmother.

"And I'm glad to be here, Mrs. Williams," David replied.

"Mrs. Williams?" Grandma Williams repeated. "Why do you call her that? It makes her sound like a matron in a boys' school. You should call her mum, David. That's what she is while you're over here."

There was silence and David looked at the floor, embarrassed.

"No, David's mum is in England," Mrs. Williams said. "Ted and I will try to be parents to him, but we can't replace his own mum and dad."

"So what should he call you then?" Grandma Williams asked.

"Uncle and auntie would be fine with us — if he wants to."

"Well, there you are," Grandma said briskly. "So now you know, David. It sounds a lot better to me."

156

"I think I'd like that — Auntie Mary," David said.

Soon it was time for dinner. The meal was grand and took a long time to eat. Bob and David ate happily, although they began to get impatient as the meal wore on.

"Well, I suppose we should open the presents," Mr. Williams announced as he lit his Christmas cigar. The adults were settling down to drink their coffee.

The boys jumped up and rushed to hand out the gifts. David read the cards while Bob took the parcels to his relatives. Mrs. Williams was delighted with the sewing basket and showed it proudly to everyone. At last the boys were free to open their own gifts.

Sitting on the floor among the wrappings, Bob picked up a square, light parcel. It was from David.

"Is it a book?" Bob asked.

"Well," David whispered, "I did think of giving you *Rusty Bedsprings* by I.P. Nitely."

Bob laughed as he tore the wrappings from the box and opened it. Inside was a model Hurricane, powered by an elastic-driven propeller.

"It's supposed to fly," David said. "Danny helped me; I did it at his place. We used one of those Model-craft kits."

"It's swell, David."

"It's got the same markings as Fred's. Danny showed me the photos."

"Look what David gave me," Bob called out, and he held up the model plane.

Mrs. Williams smiled and turned to her husband. "You know, dear, I believe it might work after all."

"They do seem to be getting on a bit better," Mr. Williams agreed.

"I'll be back in a minute," Bob said to David, and he ran up to Aunt Peg's room to get David's present from under her bed.

"I had it hidden," he said to David when he handed it to him. "They're kind of hard to wrap."

"Thanks, Bob. It looks like some sort of..." David hesitated, "...bat." David tore the paper off the hockey stick. "Gloves as well. Gosh, thanks."

"Yeah, well I thought with all that work you've been doing on your skating, you could use your own stuff."

"That's super. Shall we go and try it out?"

Bob nodded, "Sure!"

Bob and David slipped out of the front room. They took their skates from the hooks in the back porch and went out into the yard.

"Let's go, Hockeybat. It's time you learned a few moves from the master."

"Who do you think you are — Syl Apps?"

The boys went down the path laughing.